Praise for Longleaf

"During my years of roaming Alabama's backcountry, I've enjoyed many long treks through the vast longleaf wildlands of the Conecuh National Forest. For me, reading this book is as close as I can come to being there without getting sand in my boots. *Longleaf* brings to life the amazing wild critters and the secret hidden realms that make this forest a land of adventure."

— DR. DOUG PHILLIPS, host, *Discovering Alabama*

"*Longleaf* is the action-packed story of two teenagers fleeing for their lives deep in the piney woods of Alabama's Conecuh Forest. Reid has created a real hero in fourteen-year-old Jason Caldwell, seemingly a know-it-all who is bested by fifteen-year-old Leah. As the mystery unfolds, Jason and Leah must pool their knowledge of the forest environment to escape their would-be captors. *Longleaf* is filled with humor and witty dialogue and infused with tidbits of wisdom from the natural world. Let us hope Reid will take Jason and Leah on another Alabama outdoor adventure."

— VIRGINIA POUNDS BROWN,
author of *Mother & Me* and *The Gold Disc of Coosa*

"Lively characters and fast-paced action draw you right along through South Alabama's Conecuh National Forest so engagingly that you will want to devour *Longleaf* in one sitting, but force yourself to savor every chapter of this book. Enjoy a rollicking good story and learn about a unique ecosystem at the same time."

— BILLY MOORE,
author of *Cracker's Mule* and *Little Brother Real Snake*

LONGLEAF

ROGER REID

NEWSOUTH BOOKS
Montgomery

NewSouth Books
105 South Court Street
Montgomery, AL 36104

Library of Congress Control Number: 2014939910

ISBN 978-1-58838-311-2 (paperback)
ISBN 978-1-60306-098-1 (ebook)
ISBN 978-1-58838-194-1 (hardcover)

Library of Congress Cataloging-in-Publication Data
(from hardcover edition)

Reid, Roger.
Longleaf / Roger Reid.
p. cm.
Summary: When fourteen-year-old Jason accompanies his scientist parents on a trip to the Conecuh National Forest in Alabama, he witnesses
a crime being committed and finds his own life endangered as a result.

[1. Forest ecology—Fiction. 2. Ecology—Fiction.
3. Survival—Fiction. 4. Criminals—Fiction. 5. Longleaf pine—
Fiction. 6. Conecuh National Forest (Ala.)—Fiction.]   I. Title.
PZ7.R27333Lo 2006
[Fic]—dc22

Design by Brian Seidman
Printed in the United States of America

Learn more about *Longleaf* at
http://www.newsouthbooks.com/rogerreid
http://www.rogerreidbooks.com

For Ben

LONGLEAF

1

FOREVER FOURTEEN

My name is Jason, and I am fourteen years old. I have always been fourteen years old. I will always be fourteen years old. Or so it seems. That's the way my parents will think of me. Even strangers will think of me as forever fourteen when they see the dates chiseled into the tombstone. My full name will be engraved there: WILLIAM JASON CALDWELL. And carved under my name will be the dates: the year of my birth and this year—the year they found my dead body out here among the longleaf pines.

Okay, so I'm not dead yet. Who knows, maybe I will live to see fifteen. It's not looking good, though. Leah and I have been wandering around in this forest for hours now. Leah is a year older than me. I'm sorry I got her into this mess, and I don't dare let on how scared I am. She's sleeping right now or at least pretending to. I'm supposed to wake her in a couple of hours so that she can stand watch while I get some sleep. We don't know where we are. Somewhere in a longleaf pine forest. We ran deeper and deeper into the forest until we could run no more and had to get some rest. I hope Carl Morris and his brothers are resting, too.

There are several things that can kill you in the long-leaf pine forest: eastern diamondback rattlesnakes, timber rattlers, cottonmouths and the occasional alligator, just to name a few of the reptiles. Bobcats are known to be in these woods, and there are rumors of black bears. I'm not saying they would kill you, I'm just saying they could if they wanted to. Then there are the fire ants, mosquitoes and ticks. So even if we somehow escape from the big critters like Carl Morris and his brothers, the West Nile virus and Lyme disease are bound to get us. Fourteen forever. Forever fourteen.

2

A WINDOW SEAT

I t started last Sunday because I had to have a window seat. We were flying into Pensacola, Florida so that we could drive up into the Conecuh National Forest where my mom hoped to photograph and record a dusky gopher frog and a Pine Barrens tree frog. My mom is a herpetologist—that's a biologist who studies reptiles and amphibians—and for her it's not enough to look at frogs in a book. She has to see and hear for herself, and so we, Mom, Dad and I, were going to spend the first full week of April camping in the national forest and listening for frogs. This might not sound like much of a spring break until you realize that my little sister had stayed behind with our grandparents. A week with nobody croaking except the frogs was going to be sweet.

The Conecuh National Forest is in Alabama on the Alabama/Florida line about fifty miles northeast of Pensacola, and I think we were flying over the Conecuh when I saw what I saw out the airplane window. The pilot had already announced our descent into Pensacola. They told us to fasten our seatbelts and put up our seats and trays. The flight attendants were collecting cups and peanut wrappers, and I had my face pressed against the glass watching out the window. My dad and I were in the next to the last row, far enough behind the wing that I had a good view of the ground below. Well, not the ground so much as the tops of trees. Lots of trees. Lots of the same kinds of trees with a carpet of emerald green tree tops that seemed to go on and on forever. It was kind of a shock to my eyes when the trees opened up around a small lake. And there at the lake were these three people pushing a vehicle of some kind into the lake. I say "people" because at the time I didn't know they were Carl Morris and his two brothers. I say "vehicle" because I couldn't tell whether it was a car or truck or what.

"Dad, look!" I screamed. "Look! Look!"

I leaned back in my seat so he could see out the window.

"The thickest carpet of pine tops I've ever seen," said my dad.

"Longleaf pines," said my mom from the seat in front of us, "an incredibly rich and diverse habitat for all sort of wild critters."

"No," I said, "didn't you see it? Those people down at that little lake . . ."

"Lake?" said Mom.

"What lake?" said Dad.

I undid my seatbelt and stood up. "Did anybody on this plane see that small lake down there in the trees?" I called out.

Heads turned throughout the plane; nobody spoke up. Dad pulled me back down into my seat. "Fasten your seatbelt," he commanded at about the same time the flight attendant showed up.

"Fasten your seatbelt," the flight attendant demanded,

"and I'll have to ask you to please refrain from yelling."

"I witnessed a crime," I said, "at least I think it was a crime. You've got to make an announcement. Maybe somebody else on the plane saw it."

Dad leaned over me and looked out my window. "Pensacola Bay," he said.

"No, back in the trees," I said.

"I have to prepare for landing," said the flight attendant. "When we land you can tell your story to the police at the airport. Do not stand up again until we come to a complete halt at the terminal gate."

"You've got to make an announcement," I said. "Get on your intercom and ask who else saw it. There were people, three of them, pushing a car or a truck or something into the lake."

The flight attendant was already gone to the back of the plane. My guess was, and I was right, he was not going to make any kind of announcement about a car or a truck or something being pushed into a lake.

3

NINETY SECONDS

Mom thinks I'm crazy; Dad's sure of it. I have to hand it to them, though they respected what I said I saw and took me right up to the first police officer they spotted after we got off the plane. She listened with one hand resting on her gun and then looked at my parents as if to say, "Is this kid crazy or what?" Instead, she said, "Anybody else on the plane see it?"

Mom and Dad shook their heads.

"Wait here," said the officer.

She left us standing. "Wait here," that's all she had to say, and I don't think anyone of the three of us moved an inch. Was it the badge? Was it the uniform? Was it the gun? What is it about a cop that makes people, most people, do exactly as they are told? I don't know, and the truth is I wasn't thinking about it then.

I was thinking about three guys—yeah, I figured they were guys—pushing a "vehicle" into a lake somewhere in Florida.

She wasn't gone long. She returned with the pilot, the co-pilot and my friend the flight attendant.

She said, "This young man witnessed a possible crime

in progress, and perhaps you can help us determine where we need to start looking."

"You, sir," she said to the flight attendant, "did you note the time when the young man created a disturbance on the airplane?"

Maybe it was the badge, maybe it was the uniform, maybe it was the gun: the flight attendant swallowed hard before he answered, "No, ma'am."

The pilot spoke up, "How long after I called for flight attendants to prepare for landing?" he asked.

"A minute, maybe two . . . or three," replied the flight attendant.

"At three hundred miles an hour, a minute or two or three covers a lot of ground," said the pilot.

"Actually," said my dad, "it was a minute and a half."

Okay, at this point I need to say that my dad is a little weird. If he says "a minute and a half" he means one minute and thirty seconds. He does not mean one minute and twenty-five seconds. He does not mean one minute and thirty-five seconds. He means one minute and thirty seconds. I've seen it all my life, and I still don't know how he does it. It must have something to do with the fact that he is an astronomer. Somehow, someway, he's just tapped into whatever it is that makes time go by as the world turns around in space.

"A minute and a half?" asked the policewoman.

"Ninety seconds," said my dad.

"And you know this how?" said the policewoman.

My dad shrugged his shoulders. He doesn't know how he does it either.

"He's an astronomer," I said.

The pilot seemed to think that was a good enough explanation. "That would put us somewhere over south Alabama," he said.

"Somewhere?" asked the policewoman.

"Probably about fifty miles to the northeast of here," said the pilot. "Lots of pine trees up there."

"Longleaf pine," said my mom.

4

CAUSE AND EFFECT

My dad doesn't believe in coincidences. According to the dictionary, a coincidence is an event that looks like it might have been arranged by somebody even though it happened by accident. In other words, a coincidence just happens. According to my dad, a coincidence cannot "just happen" because nothing in nature "just happens." It's because he's an astronomer, a scientist. He sees everything as having a cause. Cause and effect. My dad says if things "just happen" there is no reason for science, because the goal of science is to discover what makes things happen. I don't know about all of that. What I do know is that I just happened to be looking out the window of an airplane that just happened to be over the Conecuh National Forest when I just happened to see three guys pushing a vehicle of some kind into a lake that just happened to be visible among the longleaf pines. And, oh, by the way, the Conecuh National Forest "just happened" to be where we were going

The Pensacola policewoman contacted the Covington County, Alabama Sheriff's Department and told them what this kid on an airplane "happened" to see as he flew over their area. She made arrangements for a deputy to meet us out in front of the Best Western motel which she said was in the town of Andalusia, Alabama. "Stay on US Highway 29 going into Andalusia," she said, "Best Western'll be on your right."

We picked up a rental car at the Pensacola airport and headed northeast. Mom was driving, and every now and then I would catch a glimpse of her in the rear view mirror. She did not look happy. Andalusia was on the other side of the national forest, and she was not thrilled about this delay in her expedition. The good news is that US Highway 29 took us straight through parts of the Conecuh National Forest. This seemed to cheer Mom up a bit, although she still didn't say anything. Most of the time when we enter a new area, Mom likes to tell us all about it. She kept quiet this time. So did Dad. So did I.

Seeing these trees at ground level was kind of strange. A couple of hours before I had been looking down on them; now here I was looking up. That emerald green carpet I had seen from the sky was still in the sky. I mean, these trees had no limbs and no pine needles near the bottom or even the middle of the tree. All of the limbs, all of the needles, all of the green didn't start until about three fourths of the way up. And every single tree was tall and straight. I had never seen anything like it. Tall. It was as if every tree was the same age, and not one tree was any taller or shorter than any other tree. And straight. I'm used to trees that are bigger at the bottom and smaller at the top. These longleaf pines . . . they started off at one size near the ground and ended up the same size near the sky. And just like they were all the same height, they were all the same size around. I'm not saying that they were all the same. Each tree seemed to have its own personal space a respectful distance from every other tree. Maybe it was this space between them that made each one different from all the rest.

Without warning the trees were gone. Highway 29 had carried us out of the Conecuh and where there once was forest there now was treeless pasture. The shock to my eyes reminded me of how I felt as we flew over the treetops and the trees opened up around that small lake. Wish I'd never seen that lake. We could be setting up camp; instead we were headed to a Best Western to meet a county deputy sheriff so I could tell him a story that even I was beginning to doubt.

5

DON'T CALL ME SHIRLEY

The Covington County deputy sheriff met us out in front of the motel. His name was Shirley Pickens. That's right, his name was Shirley. In fourteen years I've never met a man named Shirley. My dad says in forty-two years he's never met a man named Shirley. Here he was, though: Deputy Shirley Pickens. He had the uniform, he had the badge, he had the gun, and he had the name. Shirley. Didn't look like a Shirley. He was at least six feet four inches tall, at least two hundred and thirty pounds. And this was no baby fat. This was like two hundred and thirty pounds of "I'm going to knock you on your backside if you call me Shirley."

And yet his name was Shirley. He introduced himself that way, "Shirley Pickens."

"So you saw this 'event' from an airplane widow?" Deputy Shirley Pickens was asking me, "an airplane doing about three hundred miles an hour at about five thousand feet. Do you know how high five thousand feet is?"

I didn't answer. I was still stuck on his name. Shirley.

My dad jumped in to help me out, "Five thousand feet would be point nine five miles or one thousand five hundred twenty four meters or one point five two four kilometers—give or take."

"Well, Professor," said Deputy Shirley Pickens, "you're pretty quick with numbers."

When he called my dad "Professor," I thought he was being a smart aleck; my dad said, "How did you know I was a professor?"

"One point five two four kilometers?" said Deputy Shirley Pickens. "You're either a professor or a know-it-all, and you strike me as a nice enough guy. What about this fellow?" He looked right at me when he said, "this fellow."

"He's all right," said my dad, "but I think he's a bit intimidated by the badge and the gun and a man named Shirley."

"It does sort of take 'em off guard," said Deputy Shirley Pickens. "Sometimes they're laughin' so hard I can get the handcuffs on 'em before they realize what's happenin'."

He looked right at me when he said "handcuffs."

I know my face was red. It had to be. I gulped, "I didn't see it for long," I said, "I just know I saw what I saw. Three guys . . . three people pushing a vehicle of some kind into a small lake. I guess it was small—everything looks small from five thousand feet. Maybe I shouldn't have said anything."

"Son," said Deputy Pickens, "you did the right thing. I wish more citizens would come forward—courageously—as you have today."

"Courageously." He looked right at me when he said, "courageously."

Deputy Pickens went on to say, "Look, I know pretty near every lake, small or otherwise, in this county and half the other counties around here. I'll check it out."

My mom said, "We'll be at the Open Pond campgrounds in the national forest all week. You'll let us know what you find out, won't you?"

This was Mom's way of saying, "Let's get out of here and set up camp."

Deputy Pickens agreed to keep us informed, and we headed to the camp site. I figured that was the end of it as far as I was concerned. I figured wrong.

6

GATOR BAIT

The sign said DO NOT FEED THE ALLIGATORS. Underneath someone had taken a Sharpie and written, "your leg."

Do not feed the alligators your leg. Good advice. I spent a little time on the Internet trying to find out about the Conecuh National Forest before our trip. You know what it's like, you start out with a simple search and one thing leads to another which leads to another which leads to another, and before you know it, you've got way too much information. I knew I had way too much information when I read about the man who had his leg ripped off by an alligator at the Open Pond Recreation Area. The Open Pond Recreation Area was where we set up our base camp.

Everything you read about alligators tells you something like, "Attacks on humans are rare." I'm sure that's what the one-legged man thought. Everything you read also tells you that alligators are "carnivorous" and "opportunistic" feeders. In other words, they'll eat anything that gets too close as long as it's meat. Gators will lurk at a water's edge and can lunge about five feet to snatch an unsuspecting prey. That prey includes fish, turtles, birds, and even other alligators. And guess what? They enjoy a tasty mammal. You know, "mammals," those hairy, warm-blooded animals like squirrels, raccoons, beavers, dogs, cats and me. Gators are America's largest reptiles, and they are not considered "large" until they get to be seven or eight feet long. They can get up to fourteen feet or more and weigh a thousand pounds. When they get that big, they like to attack their prey by grabbing a leg or an arm and spinning until they rip it off.

Most alligator attacks happen in south Florida. Experts say that's because humans keep moving into the gators' natural habitat. The gators learn to adapt. Some have been seen climbing fences to get at pets. I couldn't help wondering how the Conecuh alligators have adapted to people setting up nylon tents in their habitat around Open Pond.

Maybe I worry too much. According to what I read, gators get sluggish and don't eat when temperatures get down around seventy degrees. When it starts to get cold, they burrow a hole in the ground and crawl in. They lie still and quiet until it warms up again. That's because they are reptiles, and reptiles are cold blooded. Cold blooded animals have their body temperature regulated by the temperature of the world around them. When the temperature outside goes down, the temperature inside the gator goes down. When the temperature outside goes up . . . you get the idea. Seventy degrees or so seems to be temperature where they slow down to the point they don't eat. Here at the Conecuh in early April the temperature is what? Yep. Seventy degrees. So are the gators waking up? Are they hungry after dozing in a hole in the ground for four months? Have they been dreaming of that first springtime meal? Perhaps a tasty, warm-blooded mammal?

No. Not to hear my mother the herpetologist tell it. She says, "The alligators will not be active and feeding until temperatures reach above twenty-seven degrees Celsius and maintain that temperature over a period of days."

For those of us who are not biologists, she meant to say, "The alligators will be out looking for something to eat when it gets into the eighties."

Okay, this means I should not have to worry about alligators during the first week of April. Still, when I saw the sign that read,

DO NOT FEED THE ALLIGATORS

YOUR LEG

I sort of missed my little sister. She's smaller than me and not as fast.

7

LEAH

We set up our base camp at the Open Pond campsite, and then I took off to get the lay of the land while there were still a couple of hours of daylight left. Open Pond is the largest of a series of lakes in the area. There are a couple of smaller lakes, or "ponds" as they call them down there, named Ditch Pond and Buck Pond. Then there are even smaller ponds that may or may not have names. Each pond is separated from the next by sandy soils and longleaf pines. Thick, aquatic grasses run out about ten feet from the banks and around the entire borders of the ponds. At Buck Pond, a wooden fishing pier extends from the bank to the outer edges of the aquatic grasses and then makes a "T" so you can stand and fish. The pier is about six inches above the water, and I would guess a heavy rain could send water right over the top of it.

I was standing on the bank, looking at the pier and thinking how impossible it would be to spot an alligator in the thick weeds and how an alligator can lunge up to five feet with no warning and how alligators in south Florida have been seen climbing fences, when a girl yelled, "Take a picture; it'll last longer!"

The girl thought I was staring at her.

I tried to explain that I was just trying to spot an alligator in the aquatic grasses.

"Aquatic grasses?" she said. "Weeds is what they are, water weeds. You ain't got to be scared o' gators? Too cool for gators."

"I'm not scared of gators," I told her. "I'm just wondering, that's all."

"Come back in May," the girl said. "Gators get their spring fever in May. You wonderin' 'bout gators, come back in May, if you ain't scared." She turned her back to me and started tossing bread into the water.

She turned her back on me.

I strolled out on to the pier and said, "Of course I'm not scared of alligators. Besides, everybody knows alligators don't become active and start feeding until the temperature gets above twenty-seven degrees Celsius for a few days."

"Twenty-seven degrees Celsius? What-n-the-hell are you talkin' about?" she exclaimed.

Hell? She said "hell." If I said "hell" I would get an hour long lecture from each parent explaining how cursing is the way of the "uneducated mind." A mind "lacking the vocabulary for more appropriate descriptive terms." That would be an hour from each parent. Two hours. It would be easier on all of us if they would just wash my mouth out with soap.

"Hell," I said, "twenty-seven degrees Celsius is eighty-something degrees Fahrenheit. Everybody knows that."

"Everybody?" she said. Long, thick, shaggy, black hair seemed to swirl in slow-motion as she spun around to confront me. She said again, "Everybody?"

It was not a question I wanted to answer at that point. What I wanted to do was jump into the water weeds and disappear.

The girl was about my height, maybe an inch or two taller. She was wearing cut-off jeans that came down almost to her knees and a red and white Christmassy-looking sweater that seemed out of place in the spring green of the Conecuh. She wore black Converse Chuck Taylor All Stars and blue socks. She looked me right in the eye and said, "My name's Leah. I'm fifteen years old. And you are?"

I told her my name and didn't mention my age. Well, if I couldn't impress her with my age, I would impress her with my vast knowledge. I spent the next ten minutes or so telling this girl everything she needed to know about alligators.

She was polite enough as she listened. When I was through she said, "You ain't never seen a gator out in the wild, have you?"

"My mom's a herpetologist," I said.

"You ain't never seen a gator out in the wild," she said again. "Come back in May. That's when gators get their spring fever. If you ain't scared."

"Me? Scared?" I said. Then I made that joke about coming back with my little sister as gator bait.

Leah said, "I can't believe you'd say something like that. That's mean."

"You don't know my little sister," I said. "She'd make excellent gator bait."

"I bet I can out run you," Leah said. "Maybe I just leave

you here for gator bait."

And she proved it. She took off, and I've never seen anyone run that fast. I ran after her for about twenty yards before I realized I was embarrassing myself. I called after her, "I was kidding." I don't think she heard me. I think she outran the sound.

8

PERCHANCE TO DREAM

There are sounds in the Conecuh National Forest night that will make the hair on the back of your neck stand up. I didn't hear any of those sounds that first night. All I heard were air conditioners. Yep. Out in the middle of Nowhere, Alabama about as far from civilization as you can get in the southeastern United States and I'm not hearing bobcats. I'm not hearing frogs. I'm not hearing night owls. I'm hearing air conditioners. About three-fourths of the Open Pond camp sites have water and electrical hookups for RVs, and about three-fourths of those were full. That means about twenty-five motor homes, urban sprawl on wheels, filled the air with the hum of air conditioners. Mom promised we would be spending the following nights at different frog ponds away from the main campground. That first night we would have to try and get to sleep with the whirr of climate controlled camping.

To make matters worse, there was that girl. Leah. She turned her back on me. She said things like "ain't" and "hell." Did she know Celsius from Fahrenheit? I don't think so. How could she run so fast? Maybe because there was no brain in that head to slow her down. "Come back in May

if you ain't scared," she said. Hell, I ain't scared. And why
did she have to be a year older than me? She couldn't be
thirteen; she had to be fifteen. One lousy year. Never seen
eyes like hers. Dark, dark, dark eyes. Some kind of Alabama
voodoo eyes. I didn't know they had voodoo in Alabama.
Leah? What kind of name is that?

I must have dozed off around midnight. It was not
a restful sleep. I had too much to dream. In outer space.
Alone. Quiet it was except for the drone of the spacecraft's
life support systems. Weightless, I drifted up to a porthole
and looked down upon this strange new world. It was not
the blue planet. Not mother earth. Green. Everything was
green. The green planet. In my dream I wanted to go there.
To the green world. There was something for me in the
green world; I just didn't know how to get there. Then I
heard the voices.

"Shut up," said the first voice.

"You shut up," said the second voice.

"Both of you shut up," said the third voice. The third
voice sounded like it was in charge.

The voices were coming toward me. "How you know
this is it?" asked one of the voices.

The voice in charge said, "You ain't gone fly in no airplane
with no motor home."

Then there was a voice I recognized. My dad said, "Hello?
Who's there?"

This voice—my dad's voice—woke me up. I sat straight
up in my sleeping bag. My dad was sitting up, too.

Mom snuggled her bag up under her chin. "Let me sleep,
please," she said. "We'll be up all night tomorrow."

Dad looked at me through the darkness. "Did you hear them?" he whispered.

I shrugged my shoulders.

"Probably a couple of drunks who couldn't find their own tent," he said.

9

THREE STOOGES

I woke up thinking about what my dad had said, "A couple of drunks who couldn't find their own tent." Maybe I did hear voices. Real voices. That morning I was hearing real voices. My mom's, my dad's and another voice that sounded familiar. I crawled out of my sleeping bag and unzipped the tent. Our tent was on a slight slope that dropped off toward Open Pond. Down close to the water's edge was a picnic table, and the morning sun was reflecting off of the water so that all I could see were the silhouettes of three people sitting at the table. I could tell from the voices and the shapes that one of them was my mother, one my dad, and the other was . . . Deputy Shirley Pickens. That shape, that voice. Yep, it was the deputy.

I slipped back into the tent and decked myself out for a day in the forest: heavy nylon olive green pants with zip-off legs, a sandy-colored nylon shirt, synthetic wool hiking socks and waterproof leather boots. Then I joined the group at the table. They were all drinking coffee. They didn't offer me any.

"I guess you're right, Professor," Deputy Shirley Pickens was saying to my dad, "probably some drunks who couldn't find their way back to their own tent."

"So, we did hear voices last night?" I said.

"Your mother didn't, but I did," said Dad. "Sounded like the Three Stooges coming through the campgrounds. I thought they were about to get into the tent with us."

I looked around the campgrounds. I counted twenty-five motor homes. I counted one tent.

"Do you notice anything?" I asked.

And then I answered my own question, "There is one tent out here, and it's ours."

Mom, Dad and Deputy Pickens looked around to confirm my claim.

"Lot of tents on the other side of the lake," said the deputy. "The unimproved tent sites are on the other side of the lake."

"We had to set up our base camp here at the RV sites," said my mom. "Had to have electricity for my PowerBook."

"You think those Three Stooges were on the wrong side of the lake?" Dad asked the deputy.

"Yeah," he answered, "if you ain't used to the longleaf you can get out there in the forest and it all looks the same, 'specially at night. Come in at night and you wouldn't know which side of this lake you on."

Deputy Pickens stood up, finished off his coffee and set the cup on the table. "Thanks for the coffee," he said to my parents.

He turned to me. "Young man," he said, "I told your folks that so far I ain't turned up nothin', but I'm still lookin'."

I nodded. "Thanks for letting us know," I said.

"You think of anything else, you let me know," he said. "See you folks later."

Deputy Pickens tipped his hat and walked away. His patrol car was parked on the road up the slope and past our tent. I watched as he paused just above our tent and seemed to study the sandy ground. He squatted down for a closer look. When he stood back up, he took a glimpse back toward me. I don't know if he could see my face with the sun behind me like it was. I waved. He made a slight wave back and then took his foot and shuffled up the ground where he had been looking.

"Orange juice?" said my dad.

He startled me. I spun around to see him rummaging through the cooler.

I glanced back over my shoulder to catch another peek of Deputy Pickens. He had reached his car and paused to stare out into the longleaf pine forest. As he was turning to look back toward me again, I twisted around to my dad.

"Orange juice would be good," I said.

10

EVERY DIRECTION

Covington County Deputy Shirley Pickens was correct: if you're not used to the longleaf, you can get out in the forest and it all looks the same. That's another way of saying it's easy to get lost in a longleaf pine forest. I know it for a fact. After the deputy left that morning, I went right out and got myself lost among the pines. Here's how it happened.

I sipped my orange juice and listened until I heard the deputy drive away. Even then I waited five minutes or so before I got up and walked over to where I had seen him examining the ground. What had he been looking for? It was kind of hard to tell in the soft sandy soil. Every few feet or so I could see what looked like a footprint. I guessed the deputy had seen the footprints of those guys my dad called the Three Stooges. The deputy had stirred up the ground with his foot and had erased some of the obvious footprints nearest to our tent. I guessed he just didn't want us to know how close the Three Stooges had come. A few feet up the slope from the tent I was able to pick up a trail of prints that carried up to and across the road and into the forest. The trail of footprints ended where it entered the forest.

Pine needles don't capture footprints the way sand does. In fact, pine needles don't seem to capture footprints at all. I thought maybe I could find some evidence of the Three Stooges by looking for pinecones or ferns that had been crushed under the weight of someone's foot. I stepped from the road and across the threshold of the longleaf forest. I guess I had my head down following what I thought were clues: a broken fern limb here, a flattened pinecone there. Once I spotted a fire ant bed that looked like it had been stepped in. Watching the ground is not the best way to keep oriented to where you are. After a while—it could've been ten minutes, could've been twenty minutes, could've been thirty minutes, I don't know—I just know that after a while I looked up and everything looked the same. I had been following what I thought were clues, and now I had no clue where I was.

In every direction the tall longleaf pines reached up toward the sky. I had seen this forest from an airplane as we approached Pensacola. I had seen this forest from a car as we drove to Andalusia. Now, here I was right in the middle of it. And in every direction I looked I saw tall, longleaf pines, and that's it. I didn't see oaks. I didn't see beech. I didn't see poplars or sycamore or hickory or even other species of pine trees. Longleaf pines. That's all. Each tree seemed to be about twenty feet from the trees around it. This distance between the trees allowed for a line of sight through the forest for about fifty yards or so. It was like looking through a tunnel, well, not so much a tunnel as a corridor—a corridor with straight, tall walls. At the end of the corridor, the tall pines came together, and from where

I stood it looked like the end of the line. I took a few steps forward, and the whole corridor moved with me. A step to my right and, yep, the corridor turned with me. In every direction the forest opened up in front of me then closed about fifty yards away . . . at the end of the line.

11

WALL TO WALL

I n our tent down at the Open Pond Recreation Area there was a nice Kelty daypack loaded with everything a guy would need for a hike through the longleaf pines of the Conecuh National Forest. A great bag full of great stuff—my stuff—and it wasn't doing me a bit of good. In that pack was clean water, granola bars, a watch, a signaling mirror, waterproof matches, a space blanket, a first aid kit, a whistle you could blow in case you got lost, and a compass you could use to make sure you didn't get lost. There are three hundred sixty degrees on that compass; that's three hundred sixty different directions. One of those directions would take me back to camp, and maybe forty of them would get me close enough that I could find the camp. That still left three hundred twenty wrong directions I could take. No sense taking a step in any direction when for every one right step there could be eight wrong steps. I checked the ground for ants, sat down in the pine straw and leaned my back against a tree.

Maybe if I stay quiet and listen I can hear those motor home air conditioners, I thought. Nope, all I heard were the motors of the forest. That's what it sounded like. Motors.

I've read books and stories where they describe the sounds of a forest in musical terms: the song of the whippoorwill, a symphony of crickets, the ballad of bees, things like that. In the longleaf forest at mid-morning, the birds and the bugs didn't seem to be making music; they were all business. Millions of organic motors were revving up and drowning out any hope I might have of hearing the electric motors back at the campgrounds. I heard one of those living engines fly in over my head while making a rapid-fire chirping sound.

It was a bird about six or seven inches tall and about equal parts black and white. A black top sort of looked like a cap sitting up on its head. It had white cheeks separated from its white belly by a black stripe that seemed to run from its beak into its wings. The wings and its back were black with white zigzags. I didn't know what it was at the time and figured I would look it up in one of my mom's bird books when I got back to camp. The bird was clinging to the side of a longleaf pine. It would hop around for a few seconds, pause, cock its head toward me and then go into this clattering squeak. Judging by the fuss it was raising, it wasn't happy about me being there. "I'm not happy about it either," I told the bird. It flew away.

They say that if you're lost you should quit moving and wait to be found. If you keep moving, they say, you'll get more lost and might be moving away from your rescuers. Sitting still until I was found might work, I thought. My parents would wonder where I was. They would look for me. When they couldn't find me, they would call in the Forest Service, maybe the local fire and rescue folks, maybe the local sheriff's department. I imagined Sheriff's Deputy

Shirley Pickens searching for me and wondering why he had ever called me "courageous."

"Son, you did the right thing. I wish more citizens would come forward—courageously—as you have today." That's what Deputy Pickens had said the day before. What would he say if he had to search for me in the woods?

Besides, I thought, it would be evening before my parents realized I wasn't coming back. I could be out in the pines all night if I sat there waiting to be rescued.

Walls of trees boxed me in with three hundred twenty wrong directions and a wall of noise blocked me out of hearing any hint where the campgrounds might be. Okay, if I couldn't see my way out, if I couldn't hear my way out, I would have to think my way out.

12

MAP MAKING

Think. Think. Think. Think.

Okay, when I woke up that morning and looked outside the tent I saw the silhouettes of my mom, my dad and the deputy down by the lake. That means the sun was behind them. That means I was looking to the southeast. And that means when I walked away from the water, past the tent and into the forest, I was moving from southeast to northwest. I looked to the sky. From where I sat in the pine straw, the sun was in front of me and to the left. That would be southeast, I thought. It was still morning, so the sun would still be to the east. It was early spring, so the sun would still be somewhat to the south. So I knew where southeast was, and I knew the lake was southeast of my tent. So what? All this meant was that if I were at the tent, I could find the lake. Big deal. It still didn't tell me how to get out of the woods, because I didn't know what direction or directions I had taken once I got into the woods.

Think. Think. Think. Think.

Okay, we had driven from Pensacola, Florida to Andalusia, Alabama. "Stay on US Highway 29," the policewoman at the airport had told us. That means the highway was running from the southwest to the northeast. The highway had taken us through the national forest, so it must have been running more or less northeast through the forest. When we left Andalusia we followed US 29 back into the forest—we would have been going southwest at that time. We turned left onto another road that took us deeper into the forest. So if we turned left off of a road going southwest, that means we would have been going more to the south or a little to the southeast. We turned left again off of that road, so then we would have been going east and maybe somewhat north. Then we traveled a short distance and turned right into the Open Pond Recreation Area. I was beginning to confuse myself.

Think. Think. Think. Think.

I cleared away a patch of pine straw and tried to draw a map in the dirt. I sketched out the roads as best I could. Looking at my simple map it occurred to me that I had not crossed any roads since I had been lost. That meant, I thought, if I walked north, sooner or later I would run into Highway 29 again. With any luck, I would hit the road to the campground long before that. I picked myself up from the ground, dusted myself off and headed out with the sun over my right shoulder.

"You goin' the wrong way," said a girl's voice.

I screamed. I didn't want to scream. I had no choice.

"You lost, ain't you?" the girl said. It was that girl from the pond the day before. It was Leah.

I wanted to hear myself say, "No." All I heard was my own heart pounding in my ears.

"Didn' mean to scare you," she said.

There was no denying it. She had heard me scream. Now I was standing there unable to speak. My chest was heaving, and I was thinking how lucky I was that I hadn't peed in my pants. I took a quick glance down just to be sure.

That morning she was wearing cut-offs that were half-way up her thigh, and she had on a bluish-green shirt that looked like it might have been handed down by a much larger brother. She wore the All Stars with red socks. She walked over to my crude map. "Pretty good," she said.

She kneeled down and pointed to my lines in the dirt. "This would be Highway 29, I guess," she said. "And this would be County Road 137, making this County Road 24."

She stood and turned to me. "Not bad," she said. "Eventually you'd've found your way to Highway 29 'bout six miles north of here. You want-a go that way, or you want-a follow me to the lake? It's 'bout a quarter of a mile."

I took a deep breath and let it out.

"Follow you," I said.

13

THE DEVIL IN DENIM

L eah stopped at the edge of the forest where it was about to turn back into a campground. It was a sudden stop. An unplanned stop. Like she was about to step on a snake. Her shoulders tensed, and she held up her left hand as a signal for me to stop, too. I saw no snake. Leah stared out across the campgrounds. Her glance seemed to follow the curvature of the lake.

"There's two of 'em," she said.

"Who?" I asked her.

She pointed to a pickup on the road around the lake. "See that truck over there? Back window's busted out. Got-a piece of plastic where the window's supposed to be. It's two-toned, blue and white. Three-toned if you count the rust."

"I see it," I told her.

"That's the Morris brothers' truck. Carl Morris and his two idiot brothers. I see the two idiots down by the lake. Where's Carl?" She must have been talking to herself, because I would not have known Carl if I'd seen him.

She scanned the lake line.

"There he is," she said, "talking to that fella down near that tent."

I said, "That fellow down by the tent is my dad."

Leah spun around to face me, and like the first time I saw her, that long, thick, shaggy, black hair seemed to swirl in slow-motion. As her dark, voodoo eyes fixed on mine, the hair continued in a wave across her face. It looked like a shampoo commercial.

"Your dad," she said. It was not a question; it was a statement of fact.

"Wait here," she told me as she—and her hair—spun away from me and took off toward my dad and this Morris guy. I gave her a little head start and then took off behind her. Who did she think she was telling me to "wait here"?

Dad and Morris were at the same picnic table down near the water's edge where Deputy Pickens had visited that morning. About halfway there Leah paused. "All right, then," she said without looking at me, "come on." I stepped up alongside her, and we both strolled down to the table near the lake.

Dad had a look on his face I've seen many times. When folks find out that my dad is a physicist and an astronomer, they like to share their theories of the universe with him. That's when he gets "the look." To the untrained eye, it appears that my dad has tuned out and glazed over. No. He's practicing his own intense form of listening. Even when he thinks the speaker is full of bull, he captures the conversation with his tape recorder brain. Later he will replay it and write out the person's "Theory of Everything" in his journal. One day, according to my dad, he's going to write a book in which he uses these bizarre theories as a starting point for explaining why things cannot be the way most people think they are. It sounds like a good idea to me except for the part where you have to listen to a bunch of crackpot theories. As Leah and I approached, Dad was listening to the crackpot theories of Carl Morris.

If the devil wore denim, I'll bet he would look like Carl Morris. He had on a blue jean shirt, a blue jean jacket, and guess what? He was wearing blue jeans. He was wiry guy about five feet nine inches tall with a grungy goatee and greasy black hair. It was hard to tell how old he might be because his skin was leathery from years of too much sun. I couldn't make out what he was saying to my dad. Whatever it was, Carl Morris stopped in mid-sentence when he spotted Leah.

"Well, hey, Miss Leah," Carl Morris said, "What you doin' out here? You got a new friend. You gonna introduce me to your new friend?" He looked at me when he said "new friend."

"He's my friend, ain't your friend, Carl Morris," said Leah, "An' this fella here," she pointed to my dad, "he ain't your friend neither."

Did you ever want to be invisible? Well, at that moment I was invisible and so was my dad. It was all between Leah and Carl Morris, whatever "it" was. Dad and I kept our mouths shut.

"Aw, Miss Leah," said Carl Morris, "just cause your daddy an' my daddy don't like each other don't mean you an' me can't be friends."

"Yeah," said Leah, "yeah, it does. You need to get them two idiot brothers over there and load them in that three-toned-piece-o'-junk truck of yours and get out of here."

"Miss Leah, it ain't right to talk about a man's truck that way," said Carl Morris.

"Try not to run over any deer or turkey on your way out," said Leah. "You know how the game warden feels about killin' when it ain't huntin' season."

When she mentioned the game warden, Carl Morris straightened up.

He turned to my dad, "Mister?"

"Caldwell," said my dad.

"Mr. Caldwell," said Carl Morris, "good talkin' to you."

We watched as he collected his two brothers and drove away. When they were gone, I asked Leah, "So how come your dad and his dad don't like each other?"

"'Cause my daddy shot his daddy," she replied.

14

VOODOO SCIENCE

The scientific method is most often defined as a four step process of discovery.

Step 1: Observation. In this step you take a close look at something and try to describe it as it is.

Step 2: Hypothesis. With this step you try to come up with a hypothesis—your best guess—about what causes the thing you have observed to be the way that it is.

Step 3: Prediction. This is where you stick your neck out and say, "If my hypothesis is correct, then here is what will happen when we test it by experiment." For example, say you observe a car speeding down the highway. You have a hypothesis: the car is doing sixty miles per hour. Based on that hypothesis you can make a prediction: at sixty miles per hour it will take the car one minute to go one mile.

Step 4: Experiment. Some people refer to this as the testing stage. If your hypothesis is correct, your prediction will not be proven wrong by experiments even if those experiments are conducted by people who don't believe you are correct. If that car is doing sixty miles per hour, no matter how many times you test your prediction, no matter how many different people test it, the car will always take one minute to go one mile. If it takes less than a minute or more than a minute, you need a new hypothesis.

I needed a new hypothesis.

The best hypothesis I could come up with after all my observations of Leah could not be tested. In other words, I could not begin to predict what she would do or say next. The scientific method could help unravel the mysteries of the universe. It could not help unravel the mysteries of this Alabama voodoo child.

My dad tried an end run around the scientific method.

"Why?" he asked. "Why did your daddy shoot his daddy?"

"Don't worry," said Leah, "he didn't kill him. He's in prison now."

"Your daddy's in prison?" asked my dad.

"His daddy's in prison," said Leah. "My daddy shot in self-defense."

There were many other questions to be asked. For instance, does everyone in Covington County carry a gun? Do they settle arguments down here by shooting at each other? I wanted answers to these and other questions, and I'm sure my dad did, too. So I was surprised at his next line of inquiry.

"Would you like to join us for lunch?" he asked Leah.

15

CAMOUFLAGE

J ason's mom is a biologist?" Leah asked my dad as she helped him prepare our lunch.

"She is," confirmed Dad.

"So, Jason's mom is a biologist, and his dad is an astronomer. I guess that's why he's so smart," she said.

"We think he's pretty smart," said my dad. "That's why we decided to keep him."

I should have been flattered. Here they were saying how "smart" I was. It didn't seem right. I mean, up until then this girl had implied I was dumb as a post. Now I was supposed to believe she thought I was smart?

"Jason the Genius," she said. She turned toward me when she said it and smiled. She smiled. It was the first time I had seen that. Her dark eyes brightened, and her shampoo commercial hair brushed across her lips.

I had to look away.

"Honey?" she said.

"What?" I said.

"Would you like honey with your peanut butter and bagel?"

We were having our traditional camp lunch: bagels with

peanut butter, honey and a hint of baby's butt. When we were out camping, Dad made sure we had plenty of baby wipes. We used them to clean our hands, and the wet baby powder smell stayed on my hands while I ate giving the food a slight scent, like a baby's behind just after a change of diaper.

"Yes, honey," I said.

Leah reached for the honey jar as she said, "Where is Mom the biologist now?"

"She's gone to the Forest Service office to let them know she's here," said my dad. "They said they could point out the best frog ponds on a map for her."

"I could show her the best frog ponds," said Leah. "I love to go out in the evening and listen to the frogs. I know where all the best places are to hear them."

"We wouldn't want to impose," said Dad.

"Oh, no," said Leah, "it would be my pleasure. I've always thought I might like to be a biologist. We get a lot of biologists down here in the Conecuh, you know. Most of them come to study the RCW, because it's an endangered species. I like the frogs."

"RCW?" asked my dad.

"Red-cockaded woodpecker," said Leah. "It's a little black and white bird that goes something like . . ." And then she made this rapid-fire chirping, whistling, squeaking noise that sounded just like the little black and white bird I'd seen in the woods that morning.

"That can't be a red-cockaded woodpecker," I said, "I saw a bird that sounded just like that this morning, and I didn't see a bit of red."

"If you see red," she said, "it's not an RCW. We've got all

sorts of woodpeckers around here, and you can spot red on all of them except the red-cockaded woodpecker."

"So where does it get its name?" asked my dad.

"The male has this tiny red spot of feathers on the back of its head that's almost impossible to see."

Something just wasn't right. I met this girl the day before, I followed her out of the woods that morning, and I stood there while she berated Carl Morris to the point he left the national forest. All that time she sounded like one of the Beverly Hillbillies. Now here she was giving a lesson in rare birds to my dad the professor. It ain't right.

"The woodpeckers are interesting," she said, "but I like the frogs. Every evening the male frogs gather at the pond to serenade the females. Some people think it's only a cacophony of croaking, but I think it's very romantic."

Cacophony? Did she just say cacophony?

"You sound just like Jason's mother," said my dad.

As a matter of fact, she did sound like my mother, and it was creeping me out.

My dad said, "Jason's mom's here to record frog songs so she can play them for her students."

"You know what else I like about the frogs?" she said.

Dad fell for it just like he falls for my mom's rhetorical questions.

"What?" he said.

She said, "It's the way they can blend in with their surroundings."

16

BY INVITATION

Camouflage. That's what it was. Just like those frogs she was talking about, she blended in. With me she talked and acted one way. With Carl Morris she talked and acted another way. And yet another with my dad. That wasn't the weird thing. The weird thing was that my dad was taken in by her. I could see straight through her. Why couldn't he?

My dad said, "Jason, would you like to invite your friend to join us at the frog pond this evening?"

He was kidding, right?

I said nothing. I took an oversized bite of peanut butter and honey bagel, so that my mouth would be too full to talk.

Dad said, "Jason?"

Whatever happened to not talking with your mouth full?

I mumbled, "I don't know, Dad, she might . . . I mean, we'll be out there all night. Her parents might not like her staying out in the woods all night with a bunch of strangers like us."

"I'll ask my daddy," said Leah. "I'm sure he won't mind. He likes it when I hang around with smart people like an astronomer and a biologist."

She looked at me, "Thank you for inviting me," she said. Inviting her? Did I invite her? I don't remember inviting her.

Earlier that morning when I had been lost out in the longleaf pines, I knew that I would not stay lost. I knew that somehow I could figure a way out. I could not figure a way out of having this girl join us at the frog pond. Maybe I should have been grateful. She had, after all, shown me a shortcut out of the forest. On the other hand, what was she doing there? How did she just happen to be out there in the forest where I was? And how long had she been there before she spoke up? Had she been watching me? Did she follow me out there in the first place?

I would have asked her except for one thing. If I asked, then my dad would know I had been lost.

Worse, he would know that this girl had led me back to the campgrounds.

We were cleaning up after our lunch when Mom drove up. Good, I thought, she'll see right through this girl.

"This is Jason's friend, Leah," my dad said.

Jason's friend? How did he know she was a friend of mine? He hadn't asked me.

"Good to meet you, Doctor Caldwell," said the girl.

"I'm not a doctor yet," said my mom, "but I'm working on it."

And then the girl went into her routine about wanting to be a biologist and study frogs. My mom ate it up. I couldn't believe it.

Mom laid out a couple of maps she had picked up from the Forest Service, one of the Conecuh National Forest and another showing the Conecuh Trail. On both maps someone had taken a yellow highlighter and circled this little gray spot. The gray spot was Nellie Pond.

"They told me Nellie Pond is a good frog pond," said my mom.

"It can be," said the girl. "It dries up every four or five years or so."

How did she know that? How did she know that a good frog pond is one that dries up every now and then? If it dries up, it can't support fish, and that means there are no fish to eat the tadpoles and baby frogs. I know all of this because my mom's a herpetologist. How did she know it?

The girl continued, "What the folks who told you about Nellie Pond might not know is that we have some idiots that live around here." She turned to my dad, "Idiots like that Carl Morris and his two brothers."

She said, "These idiots will catch fish at a place like Open Pond and then release them in Nellie Pond. Of course, the fish have plenty of tadpoles to eat, and they don't have a lot of competition from other fish, so they can get fairly big fairly quickly. Then the idiots—like Carl Morris and his two brothers—go back and catch them again. They think of it as their own private fishing hole, but it's not doing the frogs any good."

"No," said my mom, "no, it's not."

"I could show you a better frog pond," said the girl.

"That would be great," said my mom.

"Where is it on this map?" I said. I turned the Conecuh Trail map so that it was facing the girl. "Is your pond on this map?"

She stared at me with those voodoo eyes. I stared right

back and refused to flinch. From the corner of my eye I could see her left arm appear to levitate up from her side. Her gaze continued to fix on mine as her left hand began to float across the map. Aimless. The hand drifted as if it had no purpose. Somehow it managed to find its way into the upper right quadrant of the map where it hovered. Then there were the circles. The hand began to move in circles and spiral back toward the center of the map. The hand paused and raised up a bit as the thumb and three fingers folded under the palm leaving one finger extended. The extended finger aimed itself at a spot on the map.

"There," she said, "the best frog pond in all of the Conecuh."

My eyes and hers continued in unblinking stare. Then the girl smiled and raised her left eyebrow. She made a subtle, almost imperceptible gesture toward the map. It was an invitation to look away, and I took it.

Her finger pointed to a tiny, grayish dot on the map. I'm sure it was just my imagination, but still I couldn't help feeling like she had conjured up this frog pond. Like somehow the pond wasn't even on the map, much less in the forest, until she waved her left hand over it.

I picked the map up and studied it.

"Looks like this pond is just a few miles north of here and not too far off of the Conecuh Trail," I said. "I'll meet you there."

17

ALONE AT LAST

Sometimes alone is the best place to be.

Getting there can be tough.

I can't be alone in my room at home, for example, because I have a telephone, a TV, iPod, and a Mac with a wireless cable modem. Then there are the books. I've heard people say they like to be alone with a good book. Most of my books are full of characters, and they won't leave me alone until I'm through with the book. My sister? Louder than a cacophony of croaking frogs. I'm not saying that alone and quiet are the same thing; I'm just saying that with my sister around the house, you're never quite alone, not to mention quiet and alone.

For me, being alone means a walk in the woods. We live in a neighborhood next to an undeveloped tract of wooded land. My mom says the trees are all about thirty years old. She says that about thirty years ago the forest was clear-cut for its timber. You can still see the evidence of the old logging roads and some of those roads form parts of trails I use when I walk through the woods. I used to be able to walk a couple of miles in a big loop, then about a

year-and-a-half ago they took out about half of the trees
for an apartment complex, and I had to reroute my loop
through the remaining woods. If they chop down the last
of the trees for another development of some kind, I don't
know what I'll do—the next woods big enough to walk in
are at a state park ten miles away.

Being alone for a walk in the woods allows you to do one
of two things: think or not think. I think I think about half
of the time. I don't think I think the other half. And I seem
to have little control over whether it's a thinking walk or a
non-thinking walk. There are times when I'll start out with
a thought in mind and lose it along the way. Other times I'll
start out with nothing on my mind and wind up figuring out
something that's been bugging me for days. Who knows?

Leah seemed a little put out when I said I wanted to
hike the trail alone. It was strange. I couldn't figure out
what was going on with her. It's not like she wanted to be
around me so much as it was like she didn't trust me in her
forest. Like it was her forest. That's the way she acted. Like
maybe she was just loaning it to the Forest Service, and the
rest of us used it at her discretion. I have to admit, she had
done a good job of getting Carl Morris and his brothers out
of "her" forest that morning. And I have to admit she had
done a good job of getting me out of "her" forest when I
was lost that morning.

At one point, while I was checking to make sure I had
everything in my backpack, Leah said, "You know it's really
easy to get turned around out there in the longleaf pines."

I said, "I have a map and a compass. I won't get lost."

My dad said, "Jason spends a lot of time in the woods back home. We haven't lost him yet."

Leah looked at me, and—bless her—she didn't say a word.

I put my compass around my neck, threw my backpack across one shoulder and took another look at the trail map. The Conecuh Trail meanders for about twenty miles through the forest. From our campsite at Open Pond it would have been around seven miles to the frog pond Leah conjured up on the map. It would have taken me too long to do seven miles, so I asked my parents to drive me to where the trail crosses County Road 24. That would put me about three or four miles away from the alleged frog pond, and I would have a couple of hours of solitary exploration.

My mom drove me to the spot, and as I got out of the car she said, "Be careful. If you get off of the trail, you could step in a gopher tortoise hole."

18

KEYSTONE SPECIES

Any hopes of this being a non-thinking hike in the woods were dashed when my mom said, "If you get off of the trail, you could step in a gopher tortoise hole."

When I had been doing Internet searches on the Conecuh National Forest and south Alabama, I had focused on alligators, snakes, bobcats . . . I wanted to know what I would be up against. Now here was this new hazard: gopher tortoise holes. In spite of trying to ignore the gopher tortoise, I did come across a lot of information about it, because it's what biologists call a keystone species. A keystone species is an animal or a plant that makes life possible for a lot of other animals and plants within an ecosystem. In the longleaf pine ecosystem, the gopher tortoise contributes to his fellow critters by digging holes, and each hole is an entrance to an underground kingdom.

This underground kingdom is a burrow that may be ten feet deep and ten, twenty, thirty feet long. The tortoise digs the burrow for himself, and a lot of other creatures take advantage of his hard work by moving in with him. I remembered reading that eastern diamondbacks and even bobcats would seek shelter in these burrows, and down under the sandy soil of the longleaf forest there might be dozens of different denizens. When I was searching the Internet, I was focused on the critters and not on where they lived. Out hiking the Conecuh Trail, I wished I had paid more attention to the underground kingdom and the tortoise who created it.

"Be careful," my mother had said. She didn't say, "Stay on the trail." She said, "Be careful."

Maybe if I veered off the trail just a little bit I could spot a gopher tortoise burrow. I mean, as long as I "be careful." And am I not always careful? It's not like I was going to stick my hand down the hole. Maybe I could watch from a safe distance and see what kind of critters came and went. I had an image of the burrow as sort of a home base where everybody was safe. A place where snakes and bobcats and birds and frogs and tortoises could all dwell in harmony until they came out of the hole. Then they might bite each other's heads off.

I stopped and pulled out my map and checked my compass. It looked like I had come almost a mile since my mom dropped me off, and the trail was about to take a turn to the east and carry me past Blue Lake. Judging from the map, Blue Lake and Open Pond are about the same size, and why they call some of them lakes and some of them ponds I'll never know. Anyway, it looked like there was a spot just above the lake where I could get off of the trail and still travel parallel to it which would allow me to keep moving in the right direction. I folded up my map and headed onward.

19

BOB

B lue Lake is another national forest recreation area. It's a spot that has been adapted for people, and even if there were no people out there that day, it sort of destroyed the illusion that I was in some faraway, undiscovered back country. Don't get me wrong; I've got no problem with picnic tables and outhouses. It's just that . . . I don't know . . . it's like, on the trail I felt like a visitor in a wild kingdom. At a man-made recreation area, I imagine the wildlife feel like visitors. On the other hand, maybe the wild animals like to drop by for leftovers after a picnic.

The trail crossed above a picnic area along the upper end of the lake for a couple of hundred yards. About halfway across I paused to check out the water. In a strange way, Blue Lake looked familiar. I knew I had never been there before, so what was it? I walked down to the lake's edge to get a better look, and gazing across the water a strange sensation swept over me, making the hair on the back of my neck stand up—this could be the lake I saw those guys pushing the vehicle into the day before.

Then I heard the whistle.

My backpack's waist straps were flapping behind me as I

ran. Next time, I told myself, I'll keep the things fastened. I stuck my thumbs under the shoulder straps and pulled the pack tighter to stop it from bouncing. While this kept the pack from beating me up, it made it harder to run. When I got to the point that the trail disappeared back into the forest, I paused and took a look back toward the lake. The whistle seemed like it had come from across the water. Nothing. Nobody. I fastened my waist straps and sprinted up the trail into the woods.

My legs tried to keep up with the pounding of my heart, and after running for maybe five minutes, I had to have a break. Glancing over my shoulder I didn't see anyone or anything, so I took a quick left into the trees—careful not to step in a hole. At what I figured was a safe distance off the trail, I dropped my pack to the ground and bent over to grab my knees. My chest heaved, and all I could hear was my own pulse pounding behind my eardrums and my own gasps for breath. If someone wanted to sneak up behind me, I thought, now would be the time to do it. Then again, if someone wanted to sneak up behind me, would they have whistled?

Leah. It had to be her, I thought. Why wouldn't that girl leave me alone? Didn't I tell her I wanted a little time to myself? How did she catch up with me? She had left our campsite saying she was going to get her dad's permission to join us at the frog pond that night. She must have taken a short cut of some kind to Blue Lake where she knew I would have to pass an open area near the picnic grounds. She knew she could spot me there. Wait a minute. If she could spot me, why didn't I spot her?

I was gaining control over my breathing and losing control over my thoughts when I heard it again. That's when I knew that it wasn't Leah. It was Bob.

If you've ever heard the call of the quail, you know how I could have mistaken it for a human whistle, and you know why they call it "bobwhite." If you haven't heard the call of the quail, there's no way to describe it to you other than to say it sounds like a human whistling the name "Bob White." Mom, ever the cautious biologist, had warned me to keep an ear out for the bobwhite. I say warned, because, according to Mom, these birds build their nests on or near the ground, and if you walk up on a covey of quail in the woods, they'll fly up and scare you right out of your britches.

I pulled my water bottle from my backpack and sat down in the pine straw to take a breather. In the distance a quail called out.

"Bob White," he said.

I wondered if he was announcing his own name or calling to a friend? Either way, when everyone you know is a Bob, I guess it's hard to forget a name.

20

WITNESS

A gentle breeze drifted through the longleaf forest. It didn't come alone. With it was a whiff of something familiar. It was a pleasing scent, and I took a long breath and tried to identify it. Above me, a presence danced across the tree tops rattling the longleaf pine needles as it waltzed its way from the southwest to the northeast. I stood up and aimed my face into the breeze. It tickled the beads of sweat on my forehead. And then it was gone. Just like that. Before I could put a name to its scent, before I could recognize the tune it was dancing to, it was gone. From the southwest to the northeast, I thought, that's more or less the way I was headed. Maybe The Breeze and I would meet again.

I kneeled down and slipped my water bottle back into the side pocket of my backpack. Time to get back on the trail. I was thinking how lucky I was that no one was out there to have seen me running from a quail when my luck took a sudden turn for the worse.

"What was that?" a voice said.

"Shut up," said a second voice.

"Both of you shut up," said a third voice. This third voice

sounded like it was in charge. And this third voice was one I recognized. I'd heard it a few hours before. It was the voice of Carl Morris.

"This is why I don't take you two huntin' with me," Carl Morris said. "Both of you shut up and listen."

Were they hunting? I remembered what Leah had said earlier. "You know how the game warden feels about killin' when it ain't huntin' season," she had said. And I remembered the look on Carl Morris' face when she said it. Would they think I was a witness? Would they think I would tell the game warden? If they were hunting, they would be carrying guns. I didn't like the idea of confronting the Morris brothers with my Swiss Army knife. I slinked down on my belly in the pine straw and listened.

Far in the distance there was what sounded like a small airplane. There were no more voices. No Bob whistling to another Bob. And no sound of movement. Maybe they had stopped, or maybe I just couldn't hear their footsteps on the soft soil and pine straw. The voices had seemed to be coming from the trail—the trail I needed to take to hook up with my parents at the frog pond. I tried to remember the trail map. From where I was, or at least from where I thought I was, the frog pond should have been about a couple of miles away if I stayed on the trail. If I could cut through the woods, the pond would be closer, maybe a mile. It didn't matter. The pond was east of the trail, and I had run off the trail to the west. No matter how you looked at it I was going to have to cross the trail to get there. I waited.

And waited. How long should I give them to move on, I wondered. I glanced at my watch. Thirty minutes, I thought,

I'll give them thirty minutes and then make a break for it. Thirty minutes might not seem like such a long time unless something is crawling up your leg. I swiveled around to see that my left boot was alive with red dots.

Fire ants. I had stuck my left foot into a fire ant bed, and some of them were marching their way up my leg.

I had to sit up to get my boot off, then I had to roll up my pants to swat the ants from my leg. They didn't like it. True to their name, their bite is like fire. It's like having a flaming match head pressed into your flesh. My leg was burning up with ant bites, and I was having to try and put out the fire without making noise and drawing attention to myself.

When I got the ants off of my leg, I paused to listen and didn't hear anything. In the heat of the day, even in the spring, the forest is pretty quiet. Animals don't move around much in the heat of the day which kind of made me wonder why Carl Morris and his brothers would be hunting at such a time. Maybe they had moved on. I had to hope they had moved on.

I stood up and strapped on my backpack. My left boot was still covered with fire ants, so I picked it up by the shoestring and hobbled off toward the trail to greet whatever fate might await me.

21

FIGHTING IT OUT

L ooking back on it, maybe I should have known. I mean, flying over the Conecuh National Forest the day before I had seen *three guys* pushing a vehicle into a small lake. That night my dad and I heard voices near our tent that sounded like *three guys*. The next morning *three guys*—Carl Morris and his two brothers—were hanging around, and Carl Morris was even talking to my dad. And out on the Conecuh Trail *three guys*— the Morris brothers once again—just happened along when I thought I was alone. Maybe I should have connected the dots to the Morris brothers and the *three guys* I had seen from the airplane.

How could I have known? As far as I knew there were four people in all of Alabama who knew what I had seen: me, Mom, Dad and Deputy Shirley Pickens. I had no reason to think that anyone else knew and no reason to think that anyone might be out to get me because I was a witness to some crime. Besides, from several thousand feet up in an airplane, I sure couldn't identify anyone, so I wouldn't make much of a witness to begin with. I had no good reason to think that Carl Morris and his two brothers were the three guys I had seen from the plane.

I did have good reason to think that the Morris brothers were poachers hunting out of season.

I was hobbling through the woods with one shoe off when a couple of renegade ants made their way up the shoe-string of the boot I was carrying and bit my hand. That was it. I swung the shoe as hard as I could into a pine tree. Then I did it again. And again. And again. The plop of my shoe banging against a longleaf pine reverberated throughout the forest. "Okay, Morris brothers," I said to myself, "come and get it. I'd rather fight it out with three poachers than a million fire ants." Famous last words. The truth is I had no intention of "fighting it out" with the Morris brothers; I figured I could reason with them. There was no reasoning with a million fire ants.

After I had beaten most of the ants off against the tree, I dusted the hangers-on with my hand, slipped on my boot and headed toward the trail. At trail's edge I paused to check the map and compass. It looked like three-quarters of a mile or so north to the road where I would turn east and then south for another mile. I could be at the frog pond in about thirty minutes—less if I hustled.

I decided to hustle.

I told myself I wasn't afraid of Carl Morris and his poaching brothers. I told myself I was anxious to see my mom and dad. And Leah? At the time I was not anxious to see her at all. I was kind of hoping that her dad—the same dad who shot the Morris brothers' dad—would not give her permission to join us.

The rest of the hike to the frog pond was uneventful except for one thing. As I approached the dirt road that would take me to the east toward the pond, I heard a car coming from the east. I ducked off the trail and watched. It was not the Morris pickup. It sort of looked like a sheriff's car, and I thought that maybe Deputy Shirley Pickens was out cruising the woods looking for clues. I wondered if I should tell him how Blue Lake reminded me of the lake I had seen from the air.

22

PACING THE CAGE

The frog pond was right where it was supposed to be. And there she was. Staring at me. Like she had anticipated the exact instant when I would round the corner above the pond. She fixed her eyes on me, and although I was still maybe fifty yards away, I could tell there was a look of concern on her face. She turned to her left and began to walk along the bank of the pond. It didn't surprise me that I had beaten my parents there. It didn't surprise me that Leah had beaten me there. It didn't even surprise me that I could see no evidence of how Leah had gotten there or how she could have gotten there ahead of me. What did surprise me was the look of concern on her face.

The last half mile or so to the pond was along a dirt road that I'm guessing was an old logging road. It didn't look like it got much use any more, bushes pushed in from both sides, and the road itself was more grass than dirt. About a hundred yards from the pond, the terrain began a slight decline, forming a mini-watershed as it dropped off toward the frog pond. The road took a sharp bend to the right, and the encroaching bushes opened up a bit about fifty yards above the pond. That's where Leah had spotted me. I stood there for several minutes and watched as she walked back and forth along the bank.

The frog pond was sort of football shaped. From one pointed end to the other would have been about forty yards and across the middle was maybe twenty-five, making it a fat football. Leah's pacing didn't take her from end to end; she covered a stretch of about ten yards in the middle—about where the laces would be. She didn't look like a quarterback about to drop back and throw a perfect spiral, though. At the risk of mixing similes, she looked like a panther trapped in a cage.

I took in a deep breath and let it out.

Without looking at me, without breaking her pace, Leah called out, "You just gonna stand there?"

I took another deep breath and let it out as I walked down toward her and the pond. I got about ten feet from the invisible bars of her invisible cage and stopped. Leah had changed clothes since I had seen her a couple of hours before. I couldn't tell what color socks she wore with her black Converse All Stars, because she was wearing long, faded blues jeans. She wore an oversized Baltimore Ravens sweatshirt, and I wondered if "Ravens" was a vague reference to her hair.

"Somethin' ain't right," she said.

"This is not the right frog pond?" I said.

"Oh, it's the right frog pond. The best frog pond in all the Conecuh."

"So what's the problem?"

She stopped and turned to me, "Problem is your folks ain't here," she said.

"No big deal," I said, "they'll be here."

"Your dad's an astronomer," she said. "I'll bet he hates to be late for anything."

"Yeah, well, my mom's a biologist. The biological clock and the astronomical clock don't always tick at the same speed."

"Is that supposed to be some kind-a crack about women always bein' late?"

"No, it's supposed to be a crack about biologists. Although now that you mention it, that could explain my sister's lack of punctuality."

I smiled. Leah didn't.

"We need to head back to the campgrounds," she said.

"I just hiked three or four miles to get here from the campgrounds," I said. "They'll be here."

Leah tilted her head to the sky, closed her eyes, and let out a sigh. I never saw her draw in a breath; I just saw her let it out in a slow, steady stream. It seemed to calm her.

"We need to go," she said, "It'll be dark in 'bout an hour."

"Big deal," I said, "that's what we came here for. That's when the frogs . . .

She cut me off, "We need to go." She started up the trail as if I was supposed to fall in step behind her.

"We're better off waiting here," I said. " I saw Carl Morris and his two brothers on the Conecuh Trail."

She stopped dead in her tracks. It was that same dead in her tracks stop I had seen that morning when she spotted the Morris brothers' truck down by Open Pond. Her back was to me. She didn't bother to turn around.

"You saw 'em on your way over here?" she said.

"Well, I didn't see them," I admitted. "I heard them."

"You heard 'em?" she said with a conspicuous amount of disbelief in her tone of voice. She still hadn't turned around.

"I heard something on the trail," I explained (I didn't mention what I heard on the trail was a bobwhite quail), "so I ducked off the trail and listened. I heard the three of them arguing about hunting."

"An' you know it was the Morris brothers?" her interrogation continued; this time she turned toward me as she said it. It was not one of those melodramatic, hair spinning, shampoo commercial turns. It was a slow, deliberate turn.

I said, "Look, I heard Carl Morris' voice this morning. I know it was him. And the others? There were two others. I assumed they were his brothers."

Leah said, "That really ain't good. That really ain't good at all."

23

A MURDER OF CROWS

Maybe you're right," said Leah.

Write it down: at about four PM on the second day of my first trip to the Conecuh National Forest, Leah admitted I was right about something. Well . . . she admitted that "maybe" I was right. At least there was a possibility I was right.

"Even if your folks had car trouble, or something like that, they'll eventually come here looking for you," she said. "We might as well wait here. Besides, I don't think Carl Morris and the two idiots will bother you as long as I'm around."

"Bother me?" I said. "Why should they bother me? I don't even know the guys."

"No, obviously you don't," said Leah, "or you would realize how dangerous they can be."

"Dangerous for me—not for you," I said with as much sarcasm in my voice as I could muster.

"Oh, they dangerous for me, too," she said with a little sarcasm of her own, "but they know better than to mess with my daddy's daughter."

"Yeah, Daddy might shoot first and ask questions later,"

I said, knowing full well it was the wrong thing to say even as the words were coming out of my mouth.

"He might," said Leah. "He might shoot anybody who annoys me."

I took this as her not-so-subtle way of telling me to shut up. Oh, well, I didn't have any more to add to the conversation anyway. I dropped my backpack to the ground and found the space blanket rolled up at the bottom of it. After a couple of minutes surveying the ground to be sure there were no ant beds, I spread the blanket and sat down. Man, did it feel good to get off of my feet.

Why would the Morris brothers be dangerous to me? I figured Leah was exaggerating to make herself look like some kind of big deal. Like she was going to protect me and the whole forest from these three wicked brothers. For all I knew, Leah's daddy was just as wicked as they were. I was thinking all of this when I realized she was looking down at me, her arms folded across her chest. The blanket is five feet by seven feet. I scooted as far as possible to one side, and nodded toward the other side. Leah sat down as far on the other side as she could get and leaned back on her elbows.

"Thanks," she said.

"You're welcome," I said.

And we sat there. And sat there. And sat there.

Somewhere, not too far away, a crow was laughing at me. Of course, he could have been laughing at Leah's Baltimore Ravens sweatshirt. Ravens are close relatives of crows. I figured Mr. Crow had seen Leah out here before and knew better than to laugh at her, though. Yeah, he was laughing at me. I pretended not to notice.

"Red-cockaded woodpecker," said Leah.

"That's a crow," I said as if I knew what I was talking about.

"Listen beyond the crow," she said.

And there it was. In the distance I could hear the same rapid-fire chirping, whistling, squeaking noise I had heard in the forest that morning, the same rapid-fire chirping, whistling, squeaking noise I had heard Leah make at our camp.

"Pretty soon we won't be able to hear the RCW," said Leah, "Crow's callin' his friends and pretty soon we won't be able to hear the woodpecker 'cause there'll be a murder of crows in the trees."

She was testing me. She wanted to see if I knew that a flock of crows is called a "murder of crows." Two can play at this game, I thought.

"Gaggle?" I said.

"Geese," she said.

"Covey?" she said.

"Quail," I said.

"Pod?" I said.

"Whales," she said.

"Gam?" she said.

"A *large* school of whales," I said.

"Pride?" I said.

"Too easy," she said. "A pride of lions."

"Shrewdness?" she said.

"Shrewdness?" I said. Had she stumped me?

"I'll give you a hint," she said, "big and hairy like the Morris brothers but not nearly as ugly."

"Apes," I said, "a *shrewdness* of apes."

"There you go," she said.

The murder of crows was gathering in the trees behind us, and, just like Leah predicted, they were drowning out the red-cockaded woodpecker.

"Listen to 'em," she said, "I'll bet they laughin' at my Ravens sweatshirt."

"And all this time I thought they were laughing at me," I said.

"Ummm . . ." said Leah, "Maybe you're right."

Write it down: twice in the same day Leah said that "maybe" I was right about something. Although . . . the more I think about it, the less I see it as a compliment.

24

HOOTENANNY

aybe you were right," I said to Leah, "maybe we should head back to the campgrounds." It was after five o'clock, and I was getting worried about my parents.

"I'm sure your folks are fine," Leah said.

How did she know I was thinking about my parents? It was logical that I would be thinking about them, I guess. They were two hours late, and it would be getting dark soon. So maybe she wasn't a mind reader; maybe she was good at reading the circumstances.

She said, "They probably had car trouble, or I might have circled the wrong spot on their map."

There were a couple of different maps my mom had gotten from the Forest Service. One was the Conecuh Trail map that Leah had used to "conjure up" the frog pond. This was the map I had with me. The other map was of the whole forest. It was a smaller scale and not as detailed as the trail map, and this was the map Leah had marked for my parents. Had she circled the wrong spot on their map? I doubted it. In fact, it seemed strange to me that she would be taking some possible responsibility for Mom and Dad being late.

"We both know you didn't mark their map wrong," I said.

"Not likely," said Leah, "but I have made mistakes before. It's rare, but it happens."

The official sunset time for that day was 6:07 PM. Already the sun was sneaking behind the tall longleaf pines to the west, and the sparkle of twilight was beginning to skip across the waters of the pond. You could feel in the air a sort of anticipation of cold—like the temperature was ready to plummet the instant the sun dropped below the horizon. The sky was clear overhead, meaning it would be a cool night. Leah sat up straight on the space blanket and pulled her legs to her chest with her knees up under her chin.

"Going to be cool tonight," I said, "too cool for bugs, alligators, snakes, and I'll bet it's too cool for frogs."

Leah turned to me with a scowl on her face and raised her left index finger to her lips. "Shush," she said.

Right on cue, as if to prove her right and me wrong, a frog croaked. It was a classic frog croaking sound announcing to the pond that "Yes, we will be singing tonight."

As the sun settled down and the night settled in, more and more frogs began to tune up for the night's hootenanny. By seven o'clock, the frog-sing was in full swing, and there were so many of them vying for attention that it was impossible to separate one from the other. My mom had told me there were twenty-five to thirty species of frogs in Alabama—more than most any other state in the country. All I can say is, they must have invited some buddies up from South America. I've never heard anything like it. There were croaks, clucks, clicks, croons, chirps, chants, cackles, chuckles . . . There is not enough onomatopoeia in my vocabulary to describe the frogs I heard that night.

And loud.

Every frog was trying to out croon every other frog. You would hear what sounded like echoes, except for two things. One, there are no rocky bluffs in the Conecuh National Forest for sound to ricochet from. And two, the sound that came back to you was louder than when it left. In other words, if ten frogs called out from the west end of the pond, twenty called back from the east and another twenty joined in for good measure from the middle. Each frog, every single one of them, was crying out for the same thing: a girlfriend. This was their way of saying, "Hey, girls, look at me. I'm better than that guy." It would never occur to a frog to be subtle and play hard to get.

I turned toward Leah. "My mom would love this," I said.

She did not respond. She sat with her knees still clutched under her chin, and she rocked with a slight sway that seemed somehow in time with the syncopated rhythms of the froggy hootenanny. At that moment it made no difference to me whether she was ignoring me or whether she just couldn't hear over the frenzy of frogs. A few minutes later it would make a big difference—the difference between life and death.

25

SCREAM

D id she hear me scream?
When I left her in a tranquil trance rocking to
the rhythms of the frogs, she didn't seem to hear a
thing. I told her that I was going to step into the woods for
just a minute, and she made no comment. I sneaked from
my end of the space blanket and headed off to find a tree
where I could pee.

The moon would not be up until after nine o'clock that
night. I walked by starlight up the road that had brought me
to the frog pond. I reached the bend where it angled back
toward the west and stopped. It was so dark that I didn't
step far off of the road to relieve myself. I was zipping up
when they grabbed me.

An arm came across my chest, and a hand came across
my mouth. I bit the hand and screamed at the top of my lungs.

Foul language rode foul breath out of a foul mouth. The
arm that was around my chest released, and before I could
run it came back at me as a club. I'm sure he meant to hit me
with his fist. He missed with the fist and his forearm came
across my face and knocked me to the ground. Then there
was a knee in my back, and that same foul breath at my ear.

The foul breath said, "You scream one more time, I kill you right here."

I didn't recognize the breath; I did recognize the voice. It was the voice of Carl Morris.

"Where's the tape?" he said.

"I don't have your tape," I said.

"Shut up," said Carl Morris, and he pushed my face into the ground.

Behind me I heard a terrifying ripping sound. I didn't know what that noise was until the duct tape was being wrapped around my mouth. They wrapped it a couple of times around my mouth and then carried it up around my eyes which took it across my ears. They were wrapping me up in duct tape. Like a mummy. I would suffocate!

I twisted and squirmed as hard as I could. No use. The knee in my back pinned me harder into the dirt.

I could hear more tape being ripped from the roll. The tape came across my nose. I began to gag.

"He gone smother," said an odd voice from somewhere behind me. "Ya'll gone have to get that tape off-a his nose."

Carl Morris pulled the tape from around my nose. I drew in a deep nose-full of air and along with it came the stench of his breath.

My sense of smell was back even as my other senses were being stripped from me. The tape over my eyes and mouth was scary enough. I couldn't see. I couldn't scream. Yet it was the tape over my ears that took the nightmare to a higher level of fright. Sounds were muffled and fragmented. Like in some horrible dream, the sounds and the information they contained were just out of reach.

"Legs . . ." I heard an expressionless voice say.

Minutes later my legs were jerked out straight behind me, and my feet were taped together.

"More . . . grab . . . back . . ." a group of disjointed voices exclaimed.

My hands were pulled behind my back and taped together. My arms were so twisted that I felt like they were going to pull out of their sockets.

The pressure that had been on my back—the knee of Carl Morris—was gone all of a sudden. What a relief, I thought, until I felt a foot against my left shoulder. The foot shoved, and I was rolled over onto my back. Then they lifted me. Or tried to. One grabbed my feet, another under my arms. The one with my feet lifted too fast causing the other one to lose his grip. His hands slipped from under my arms, and I was falling until he caught me by the hair. He used my hair to pull me back up to a point where he could grab up under my arms again. All the while there was this bizarre, muffled noise: the noise of my own screams trying to escape the tape across my mouth.

They carried me, I couldn't tell how far, and threw me into the back of their pickup truck. They rolled me to the middle of the truck bed and tossed something over me. It may have been an old blanket. I don't know. I do know that it smelled almost as bad as Carl Morris' breath.

I heard the muffled sound of the tailgate closing and the muffled sound of the truck cranking. Then there was the muffled whine of the engine working its way through the gears.

One scream.

That's all I had gotten out before they taped my mouth shut.

Did she hear me scream?

There was no way for me to know, and even if she did hear, what could she do about it?

26

THE HANDS

The hands were smaller than the hands that had wrapped duct tape around my face. Smaller than the hands that had bound my arms and legs with tape. They were smaller than the hands that had hoisted me up and tossed me into the back of a pickup truck. The hands were smaller and softer.

After the blanket or sleeping bag or whatever it was covering me was pulled away, the hands rolled me over on my back. The hands felt their way around my face like I imagine a blind person feels his way around a face to identify it. Then the hands moved to my pockets. They felt around the outside of my left pocket, and, unsatisfied, moved to the right pocket where they found what they were searching for. One of the hands slipped into my right pocket and came out with my Swiss Army knife.

The blade of the knife was cool against my skin as it slid along my face. One hand held my head still while the other, the left hand, worked the knife up under the tape over my right ear. The knife rotated so that the sharp side of the blade was away from my skin, and with a sudden thrust it cut through the duct tape. The left hand, still holding the knife, began to pull tape away from my right ear, and I could feel the gentle tickle of the hair. Even with my eyes still taped shut, it was as if I could see that hair. It was black. It was long, thick, shaggy. It floated in slow motion like in a shampoo commercial.

The hair covered my face as her lips came close to my ear. "Be quiet," Leah whispered. "Be very, very quiet."

The hair floated up and away as her hands took me by the right shoulder and rolled me over on my face. It wasn't easy to hold my head up and keep from breaking my nose against the floor of the truck bed as it bounced along the forest's dirt road. Her hands felt their way down one of my arms until they found where both arms were bound by duct tape. She cut me free.

I rolled over on my back and started to sit up. Leah grabbed my head with both of her hands and pulled me to her.

"Stay down," she said, "stay down and be quiet."

Quiet was the easy part: my mouth was still covered by duct tape. And so were my eyes. I pulled the tape away from my eyes first, taking most of my eyebrows with it. Stars. So good to see stars in the sky again. That's about all I could see. The moon was not up yet, and Leah was invisible in the pitch black of the truck bed. Next I worked on the tape around my left ear. Then my mouth.

"How did you . . ." I started to say.

Leah put her hand across my mouth and her lips up to my ear. "I heard you scream," she whispered. "I barely made it to the truck as they ere driving away. Now be quiet. Be very, very quiet."

I felt Leah run her hand down my arm until she found my hand. She placed the Swiss Army knife in my hand. I pulled my knees up to my chest and used the knife to cut my legs free of tape. I folded the knife and put it back in my pocket.

Leah put a hand to my face and turned my head so that she could whisper into my ear again. "When they slow down for any reason, we have to jump out the back of this truck—straight out the back," she said.

Sounded like a good plan except for the part about slowing down. They never slowed down. If they came upon any stop signs, it was obvious they were running right through them—without slowing down. When they took a turn they took it with gusto—without slowing down. All we could do was lie there and watch the tops of longleaf pines whiz past against the starry sky.

27

A NEW PLAN

So how do you know so much about hitting people with an axe?" I asked Leah in a whisper.

"I don't know about hitting people with an axe," she whispered back. "I know about self defense."

When it became obvious the Morris brothers were not going to slow down enough for us to make a jump out of the back of the truck, we devised a new plan. It took a while, because we had to whisper, and it was hard to hear. The plastic the brothers had used to cover their broken back window made a flapping sound. It was a mixed blessing. Although it made it hard for Leah and me to communicate, it made it even more difficult for the Morris brothers to see or hear us. We figured they were not going to slow down until they came to a complete stop somewhere way out in the forest where they planed to dump me.

"They prob'ly won't kill you," Leah said. "They'll just dump you out in the middle of nowhere and hope you die before somebody finds you."

"Why?" I asked, "Why would they want me dead?"

"Cause they're idiots," was the lone answer she would give me. It seemed to be her answer to everything about the

Morris brothers. Idiots or not, there had to be more to it, and I might have argued the point if she hadn't just come to my rescue.

I can't begin to describe all of the emotions that were swirling around inside my head, not to mention my stomach. For reasons I had no explanation for, I was in mortal danger. I had been wrapped up in duct tape and tossed into the back of a beaten up old pickup flying along dirt roads in the middle of nowhere. Then Leah had freed me, sort of. She even had the foresight to grab my backpack when she came to my rescue. If we could get out of the truck alive, at least we would have some supplies.

"They prob'ly got some tools in the back of this truck," Leah whispered to me.

I felt around in the dark up against the back of the truck cab, and sure enough, there were tools. I felt a pick and a shovel. It made me shudder. Were they planning on digging a hole—a grave? Then I felt what seemed to be a wooden handle with tape wrapped around it. I followed the handle up until I felt the axe head.

"An axe," I told Leah, "I found an axe."

"Good," she said. "If you have to hit one of 'em with it, don't swing. Jab. Jab it right into his face."

We devised our new plan. A plan that involved her running and the possibility of me jabbing an axe into somebody's face.

The truck began to slow.

"Ready?" asked Leah.

"As I'll ever be," I replied.

I pulled the axe to my right side, and Leah scooted the

backpack up on my left. She pulled the stinking old blanket over me. The truck stopped. The doors opened. I could hear Leah scramble out of the back. She let out a slight yelp, drawing attention to herself.

"He's loose!" one of the brothers yelled.

"Get him!" yelled another.

I could hear running on the dirt road.

"He's cuttin' up into the woods."

"Catch him!"

I waited for what seemed like an eternity and then kicked the cover off of myself. I didn't wait long enough. There silhouetted against the starry sky was Carl Morris looking over the side of the truck at me.

I jabbed the axe right into his face. It made a horrible cracking and squishing sound. Carl Morris squealed like a hurt dog and fell down on the road. I grabbed the backpack and jumped over the side of the truck. I could see his dark form writhing on the ground, his hands clutching his face. I should have run. Instead I raised the axe over my head.

"Where's my mom and dad?" I shouted. "You tell me where my mom and dad are, or I'll bust your head wide open with this axe!"

"Camp," he muttered. "We cut their tires. We cut all their tires."

I swung the axe into the truck and shattered the glass of the driver's side window.

Then I ran. Into the forest. Into the dark, dark longleaf forest.

28

JABBED

Leah was not where she was supposed to be. The plan was for her to run from the truck when it stopped— she had already proven how much faster than me she was. When the Morris brothers chased after her, I would climb out on the driver's side and run one hundred yards straight into the woods. She would cut into the woods to the passenger side of the truck and circle around to meet me. There was no reason for them to know she was in the back of the truck. We figured all of them would chase her thinking she was me. I had the axe just in case one of them stayed behind. Jabbing instead of swinging was good advice. If I had tried to swing the axe, Carl Morris might have had time to block it. As it was he had no time to react.

I ran in a straight line from the truck counting my steps as I went. The whines of Carl Morris faded behind me. Off in the forest I could hear the other brothers yelling to one another. A good sign, I thought; they haven't caught her. When I counted a hundred strides, I stopped and kneeled down behind a pine tree. Then I threw up. All of the night's emotions had settled in my stomach, and my stomach couldn't contain them.

At that moment I was glad Leah was not around to see me get sick. She would be there. I knew she would.

In the distance there was a sudden burst of obscenities. It was a chain of vulgarities like I have never heard strung together in one sentence, if you could call it a sentence. Then I heard one of the brothers yelling, "Carl! Carl!" Carl didn't answer. I moved away from where I had thrown up and waited.

The moon still wasn't up. I checked my watch: eight thirty-nine. It had been a little after seven when I walked away from the frog pond and was captured. We must have been riding in the back of that speeding truck for over an hour, I thought. There was no telling where we were. I checked the sky. Stars, stars, stars. In the black of the forest they were the one source of light. The longleaf canopy was open enough to let some of that light reach the ground, not open enough for me to pick out constellations. There was no way for me to tell what was north, south, east or west. When the moon comes up, at least I'll know which way is east, I thought. What good would that do, though? I doubted that even Leah would know where we were, so we would have no idea which direction to take to get back to civilization.

Back toward the truck I heard a sudden outburst of voices. I couldn't make out what they were saying. I hunkered down and tried to listen. If they were back at the truck . . . Had they caught her and dragged her back? I still had the axe. Three voices. The Morris brothers. I didn't hear Leah. She would say something to let me know they had her, I thought. Unless they taped her up like they did me. I dropped my backpack to the ground and took the axe in both hands. She had saved me; it was the least I could do. I started back toward the truck.

"You goin' the wrong way," said a girl's voice in a loud whisper.

This time I didn't scream.

"You've got to quit sneaking up on me like that," I whispered back.

"Let's get out of here," Leah said, "Where's the backpack?"

I picked up the pack and slung it over my shoulder. "Let's go," I said.

"Just a second," said Leah. She drew in a deep breath and held it. Above me, among the treetops, there it was: that presence. The same presence that had danced across the longleaf pine needles that afternoon. Once again a gentle breeze tickled the beads of sweat on my forehead.

Leah let her breath out in a slow, steady stream. "Smell it?" she asked.

I sniffed the air and shook my head. "What?"

"There's a little hint of the Gulf of Mexico in the breeze," she whispered.

I sniffed again.

"That means," she continued, "the wind is coming more or less from the south, prob'ly from the southwest. We're heading east. We'll know for sure when the moon comes up. Gonna be nearly a full moon tonight. Moon puts a lot of light in this forest. We got-a get out-a here before it does."

Just then a powerful beam of light cut through the trees. We both dropped to the ground. The beam made a slow, deliberate swath over our heads. It was coming from the direction of the truck.

"Don't look," said Leah. "Your eyes will reflect the light."

"Miss Leah!" a voice called out. It was not Carl Morris; it was one of his brothers. "Miss Leah, we don't mean ya'll no harm. Ya'll come on out, an' let's work this out."

"Sounds like Carl Morris has appointed a new spokesman," whispered Leah.

"Carl may have a hard time talking," I said. "I poked him in the mouth with an axe."

Leah chuckled. "You jab or you swing?" she said.

"Jab," I said. "I jabbed."

29

IN THE SPOTLIGHT

I think one of 'em stepped in a gopher tortoise hole," Leah whispered. "They was chasin' me, and then I heard this yellin' and cussin', and then they stopped. One of 'em was screaming he'd broke his leg in a hole."

"Good," I replied, "Carl Morris has a mashed up face and can't talk for himself, and now maybe we've got one hobbled with a bad leg."

"They ain't gonna give up on findin' us." And to prove her point the spotlight swept over our heads. "They use that spotlight for huntin' deer at night," she said. "It's illegal, but that don't stop 'em."

"Don't the deer run when they see the light?" I asked.

"Naw," she said, "they just kind-a stand there starin' right into it. Sittin' ducks."

"I sort of feel like a sitting duck myself right now," I said. "Carl Morris knows I ran in this direction."

"A Morris don't know nothin'. Just keep your head down, and don't look at the light. They ain't movin'. If they knew where we was they'd be headed this way, smashed face, bad leg and all."

The new spokesman for the Morris brothers called out

to us a few more times. We decide not to answer. At last he yelled, "Okay, Miss Leah, we gone back to town an' find your daddy. We tell 'im you out here lost in the woods."

We laid low listening as the truck started and drove away. "Don't believe it," said Leah. "They tryin' to fool us."

A couple of minutes after the truck sound faded, the spotlight slashed through the trees again. A few minutes later, we could hear the truck coming back. "We gotta get outta here," I said. "Like you said, when the moon comes up this forest will be full of light."

Leah agreed, "When they stop the truck, we make a break for it. The road is to the north of us. We're goin' east."

"Why east?" I asked.

"I always wanted to visit Georgia," she said in a tone that let me know she didn't appreciate me questioning her judgment.

"The way they were driving, we could already be in Georgia for all we know," I said.

"In that case we'll stop when we hit the Atlantic Ocean," she was quick to reply.

Sounded good to me. Any plan is better than no plan. When the truck stopped we bolted.

I had an axe in one hand and the backpack slung over my shoulder. Once again, the backpack was beating me up. Why, oh why hadn't I had sense enough to strap in on my back? We didn't run so much as jog. Leah kept her head down watching the ground. At one point she stopped and threw her hands behind her motioning for me to stop. Then she pointed at the ground.

On the forest floor was a spot where what little light

there was disappeared into the ground. "Gopher hole," she whispered, "Watch your step."

We stepped around the hole and continued our jog. I thought we were making good progress until the axe in my hand began to glow.

"There they go!" I heard a Morris brother yell.

Leah made a quick turn toward me. The spotlight was aimed right at us, and we were still invisible. The axe was not. Some kind of reflecting tape was wrapped around the handle and it glowed like hot coals.

"Oh, no," said Leah. "Throw it. Throw it far as you can back up toward the road."

I heaved the axe as far as I could right back toward the spotlight. It sparkled as the light followed it.

"Know what I said about goin' to Georgia?" she said. "Forget that. We're goin' to Florida."

And with that she turned south. This time we ran. I did my best to get the pack up on my back and to keep up with her.

Four or five minutes after we started running the spotlight quit sweeping through the trees. "Burnt out," said Leah, "Big ole light like that eats up some batteries." In the distance—way off in the distance—we could hear the truck start and move. We paused and glanced back. The truck, judging from its lights, was turning around in the road. It aimed its lights in the general direction where we had been when I tossed the axe. The truck lights were not as powerful as the spotlight had been.

"They've lost us," said Leah.

"Yeah, and they've been looking into those lights," I said.

"It'll take at least thirty minutes for their eyes to adjust to the dark."

"Their eyes won't have to adjust for long," Leah said as she pointed to her right.

The moon was just beginning to expose itself beyond the trees, and it wouldn't be long before it exposed us. "We got-a make hay while the sun don't shine," she said. And with that we were off toward Florida once again.

30

JUST LUCKY

The Morris brothers' spotlight had exhausted its batteries—lucky for us, I thought. We managed to run— jog— through the forest at night without breaking a leg in a gopher tortoise burrow—lucky for us, I thought. We had some water and granola bars in my backpack—lucky for us, I thought. When we stopped for a quick water break, we didn't find ourselves standing in a fire ant bed—lucky for us, I thought. I said to Leah, "I'd say we've been lucky. Their spotlight burned out, we haven't stepped in a hole, and we haven't been eaten up by fire ants."

"If we were lucky we wouldn't be runnin' from those idiots in the first place," she said. And with that she capped the water bottle, stuck it back in my pack, and we were off again.

Luck is a strange concept. Some things can't be good luck unless they are preceded by bad luck. And one guy's good luck can be another guy's bad luck. For instance, Leah heard my scream and managed to jump into the back of the truck and unwrap me from the duct tape. Good luck for me, bad luck for her.

My dad doesn't believe in luck anymore than he believes

in coincidences. In fact, he thinks luck is just another name for coincidence. He sees everything as having a cause. Cause and effect. "Next time you consider yourself lucky," my dad says, "stop and think about the events that led you to that point. Good luck or bad luck, you'll see that a series of actions and the results of those actions have led to your so-called luck." If he was right, what series of actions led to my bad luck known as the Morris brothers?

There was one possible explanation I could think of: I had seen three guys pushing a vehicle into a lake somewhere in this forest. Three guys. Three Morris brothers. Luck had nothing to do with it. The Morris brothers had to be those three guys. I came to an abrupt halt and called to Leah in a loud whisper. She paused.

"I think I know why they're after me," I said.

Her reply surprised me, "Does it matter?"

"At this point I guess it doesn't matter," I said.

"Then let's keep moving," she said.

"Wait a minute," I said. "What matters is how they know." I told her what I had seen from the airplane. "Three guys pushing a car or a truck or something into a lake somewhere in this forest. Three guys, three Morris brothers," I continued. "They must think I'm a witness to their crime, even if there's no way I could identify them from a few thousand feet up in an airplane."

"Idiots," said Leah. "They're just too dumb to know you couldn't make them out. But you know who they are now. Let's move." She turned to go.

"Hold up," I said. "If they're as dumb as you say, how

did they know about me spotting them in the first place?"

Leah did not respond.

"Other than my parents, I told no one except the deputy sheriff," I said. "You know what that means?"

Leah still did not respond.

I said, "It means the deputy—Deputy Shirley Pickens—has to be the one who told them. He's in on it with them."

Leah's shoulders dropped. "Deputy Pickens ain't in cahoots with no Morris," she said without looking me in the eye.

"How do you know?" I said.

"Cause Deputy Pickens is my daddy," she said. "Now, let's get out-a here."

She turned and headed east into the rising moon. I took a second to tighten the pack on my back and followed after her. "I thought we were heading south," I said.

"Change of plan," she said. And she quickened her pace.

Change of plan is right, I thought. Maybe the Morris brothers weren't after me at all. Maybe they were after her. Maybe I was just the bait. Didn't she say her daddy had shot their daddy and put him in prison? This could be their way of getting even. Then again, maybe not. When Leah had blasted off at Carl Morris at our picnic table, there seemed to be genuine . . . I don't know what you would call it . . . fear? Respect? Whatever it was, it was genuine, and he responded by hitting the road just like she told him to. No, I was the one they were after. They had followed me on the Conecuh Trail, and when they didn't get me there, they waited until I was separated from her.

I called to Leah, "Stop!"

She whirled around. "Keep your voice down!"

"Look," I said, "there's one way they could know about me: Deputy Daddy had to tell them."

This time she looked me in the eye. The moon was much higher in the trees. Her eyes glowed. She said, "Daddy told 'em some kid flying in over the forest spotted them. He knew if somebody was up to no good in the forest it would be a Morris. He didn't tell 'em it was you, exactly. They figured it out on their own. Carl Morris probably figured it out when he was talking to your daddy down at Open Pond."

"Maybe they're not as dumb as you think," I said. I couldn't believe I was taking up for the Morris brothers.

"They're dumber than I think. Dumber than I can imagine. A Morris adds two and two and gets thirteen. They got lucky. A lucky guess," she was emphatic.

"Their good luck was our bad luck," I mumbled.

"We make our own luck," she said. "Let's get out of here."

31

SHADOWS

An enchanted forest. A magic kingdom. There was no way to describe the longleaf forest that didn't sound like a Disney fairy tale. The moon was waxing gibbous which means it was more than halfway to full. In fact, it would be full the following night. It was so big it seemed to brush along the crowns of the tall trees tickling the long needles into an easy sway. It would have been a magical time in an enchanted wonderland if we hadn't been running for our lives.

We zigzagged through the forest, heading south for a zig of fifteen minutes or so then turning east to give equal time to a zag. I preferred the southern trek, because I could run side by side with my shadow. In the vivid high beam of the moon, my shadow was crisp. He wore a backpack like mine, and he used his arms to propel himself along like I did. Every now and then a longleaf pine would come between us; otherwise he stayed right at my side and didn't outrun me like Leah did.

When we turned east, Mr. Shadow fell in behind me without complaint. Every now and then I would glance back, and there he was, stride for stride. Moving east the pines were taller than tall. Their own sharp shadows rushed at me across the forest floor. At about eleven o'clock, the shadows began to shorten. The moon was rising so fast you could almost watch it move across the sky. Around midnight the shadows got as short as they would get before they started to lengthen in the opposite direction. And about that same time, me and my shadow had gone as far as we could go.

I called to Leah in a loud whisper, "I've got to have a break."

She came to a halt and said, "Me, too."

We both bent over with our hands on our knees trying to catch our breath. It was somewhat comforting to see that she was as winded as I was. "You must be tired," she said, "you hiked several miles to get to the frog pond."

"That was yesterday," I joked. "Besides, I had a nice, relaxing ride in the back of a pickup truck."

Leah laughed. So did I. And the more she laughed the more I laughed. And the more I laughed the more she laughed. We were caught in a laugh loop. It wasn't that funny. Nothing about the night was funny. The laughing felt good, though. It seemed to release the pressure in my brain, in my gut, in my bones.

"Get a hold of yourself," she said, and then she laughed some more.

"I either laugh or beat my head against a tree," I said. And we both laughed some more until we were as tired from laughter as we were from running.

Leah sat down and lay in the pine straw stretching out her arms and legs and arching her back. "Better check the ground for fire ants before you get comfortable," I said.

"They can haul me away," she replied, "I can't move a muscle."

I surveyed the ground around a pine—there was plenty of moonlight—and determined it was safe enough. I took off the backpack and sat down against the tree. "Water?" I asked.

"Not right now," she said.

We sat listening to the quiet for a few minutes, then I said, "We must be miles from the nearest frog pond. I don't hear a thing."

"Listen," she whispered.

Above me I heard it again: that presence. It made my skin crawl. The first time I had heard it—felt it—it had been followed by the voices of Carl Morris and his brothers along the Conecuh Trail. The second time had been a few hours earlier when we had just escaped from the Morris gang. And now?

"Hear it?" Leah whispered.

"Like wind chimes way off in the distance," I said.

"Not that distant," she said. "Only about seventy feet away and straight up."

I looked to the sky. Even with an almost-full moon, the forest was so dark you could still see more stars than you would believe the heavens could hold. Then I let my focus drift back to the longleaf canopy—about seventy feet straight up. "The needles," I said, "that sound is coming from the wind in the pine needles."

"Not just needles," she corrected me, "southern longleaf pine needles. And you know how a dozen different people can see a dozen different shapes in a cloud? It's like that with the song of the longleaf. Everybody hears it different."

"What do you hear?" I asked her.

"Bacon frying," she replied, and I have to admit, that took me by surprise. "I'm lying in my bed, and my momma's in the kitchen frying up some eggs and bacon—beef bacon. The sound reaches me before the smell does, but soon I'll smell it, too, and then I won't be able to stay in bed no longer. Eggs and bacon and toast with lots of butter and honey. And I'm gonna wash it down with a tall glass of cold milk."

I put my head back on the tree and closed my eyes, and I could see myself having breakfast with the Pickens family. Leah was there with her mom, and Deputy Shirley Pickens was there. There were no Morris brothers, and if they did show up, Deputy Pickens had a gun. I wouldn't have to jab anybody in the face with an axe.

When I had finished my imaginary breakfast, I murmured, "Thank you."

Leah said, "You'd-a done the same for me." And I realized she wasn't talking about a make-believe meal; she was talking about the real-world fact that she had saved my life.

32

JOURNAL

O ne of 'em got a busted leg; one of 'em got a busted face," Leah said. "I think we lost 'em for the time bein'."

"You're not just saying that because you're too tired to take another step?" I asked.

"That's exactly why I'm sayin' it," she replied, "but you got-a admit, we ain't seen or heard 'em in hours."

I agreed, "And if they didn't hear us laughing, they must not be within five miles. Why don't you get some sleep, and I'll stand watch?"

"Real good idea," she said with a yawn. "Wake me in a couple of hours." She rolled over on her left side and pulled her knees up to her chest.

"You cold?" I asked her. "I've got some long johns in my backpack."

"Long johns?"

"I'm known for over packing," I admitted.

"I thought that pack was a little heavy for a four-mile hike," she chuckled.

"You'll appreciate it in the morning when we're dining on granola bars."

"Ain't bacon and eggs, but it sounds pretty good right

now," she admitted. Then she rolled over on her other side—away from me—and said, "I left the space blanket back at the frog pond. Figured they would see it when they came lookin' for us and know we'd been there."

I reached down in my pack and pulled out my beach towel and covered her with it. "You do over pack," she said, "but I guess that ain't always a bad thing. Wake me in two hours."

I sat with my back against a tree and stuck my legs straight out trying to stretch the burning out of my thighs and calves. Far off in the distance a baby wailed. No ordinary baby, this baby was evil, and he was mad. "Bobcat. He's ticked-off at somethin', ain't he?" Leah muttered. She wasn't expecting an answer, so I didn't offer one. I settled in against my tree and found my journal in the backpack. There was plenty of moonlight to write by, and I felt like I had to make a record of recent events. This is what I wrote:

> My name is Jason, and I am fourteen years old. I have always been fourteen years old. I will always be fourteen years old. Or so it seems. That's the way my parents will think of me. Even strangers will think of me as forever fourteen when they see the dates chiseled into the tombstone. My full name will be engraved there: William Jason Caldwell. And carved under my name will be the dates: the year of my birth and this year—the year they found my dead body out here among the longleaf pines.
>
> Okay, so I'm not dead yet. Who knows, maybe I will live to see fifteen. It's not looking good, though. Leah and I have been wandering around in this forest for hours now. Leah is a year older than me. I'm sorry I got her into this mess, and I

don't dare let on how scared I am. She's sleeping right now or at least pretending to. I'm supposed to wake her in a couple of hours so that she can stand watch while I get some sleep. We don't know where we are. Somewhere in a longleaf pine forest. We ran deeper and deeper into the forest until we could run no more and had to get some rest. I hope Carl Morris and his brothers are resting, too.

There are several things that can kill you in the longleaf pine forest: eastern diamondback rattlesnakes, timber rattlers, cottonmouths and the occasional alligator, just to name of few of the reptiles. Bobcats are known to be in these woods, and there are rumors of black bears. I'm not saying they would kill you, I'm just saying they could if they wanted to. Then there are the fire ants, mosquitoes and ticks. So even if we somehow escape from the big critters like Carl Morris and his brothers, the West Nile virus and Lyme disease are bound to get us. Fourteen forever. Forever fourteen.

33

WIPE OUT

Leah had far more than two hours sleep. I made sure of that by falling asleep myself and not waking until the first bird of the morning brought us both back to life.

"Is my two hours up already?" she quipped as she rubbed the sleep from her eyes.

We both stood up and stretched our arms and legs back into their proper positions. Then Leah bent over at the waist and shook her hair over the back of her head letting it fall toward the ground. "Do me a favor," she said, "check me for ticks."

When I didn't respond right away, she said, "A tick looks like a little dot with legs."

"I know what a tick is," I responded. "I was just thinking that maybe we should have a couple of granola bars and get a move on."

Without standing upright, she turned her head so that she was looking at me through her thick, black hair. I couldn't see her eyes as she spoke, "I ain't gonna bite, but I am thinkin' about kickin' your butt."

"I'm thinking it's still too cool for ticks," I babbled, "I'll bet tick season doesn't start around here until late April, maybe even May."

Leah jerked upright. If I had been standing two feet closer her flailing hair would have whipped me like a cat-o'-nine-tails. "Forget it," she said.

"I'm sorry," I said as I took a step toward her. "Here, let me . . ."

"Don't you touch me!" she demanded.

"You're right," I said, "south Alabama, as warm as it is down here there could be ticks in March, February, even."

"Just shut up and give me a granola bar," she grumbled.

We had a granola bar breakfast and washed it down with water. When I handed Leah the water she made a big show of rubbing the lip of the bottle with her sleeve before giving it back to me. There was a chill in the air that could not have been measured with a thermometer.

"I have several more granola bars," I said in a vain attempt to thaw the ice.

She did not respond. Without a word she turned and headed into the rising sun. "We're going east again this morning?" I asked.

No response.

Any other time I would have emptied and repacked my backpack to distribute the weight for a new day's hike. There was no time for that. I grabbed up the things that I had taken out and stuffed them into the bag. I did take the time to fasten the pack to my back before setting off. The pack felt lumpy against my back, and I had to fight the urge to stop and repack. If she wants to walk off and leave me, that's fine, I thought; besides, I have all the provisions.

It took a couple of hours to catch up with her. Yeah, I

could have run and caught her right away . . . but that just didn't seem like the thing to do. I set a pace that would allow me to gain on her without running. It wasn't easy; she had set a pretty swift pace of her own. And not once did she pause to catch her breath, not once did she pause to tighten a shoelace, not once did she pause to check her direction, not once did she pause to glance back and see if I was still on the planet.

After a couple of hours I was maybe ten feet behind her, and she still didn't look back. I knew she heard me gaining on her. Just to make sure, I said the first thing that popped into my head, "You're a Baltimore Ravens fan?"

"I'm an Alabama Crimson Tide fan," she replied.

"It's just you're wearing a Ravens sweatshirt," I said.

"I know what I'm wearin'," she retorted.

"You know," I said, "the team started out as the Cleveland Browns, then they moved to Baltimore and became the Ravens. The Ravens left the name 'Browns' behind so that if Cleveland got a new team they could keep their old name. So now you have a Cleveland Browns and a Baltimore Ravens."

She stopped and turned toward me. It was a curt stop and a slow turn. No swirling hair, no shampoo commercial. She said, "Can't you even make small talk without sounding like a know-it-all?"

I've been called a know-it-all before. This was the first time I can remember it bothering me.

She continued, "The Cleveland Browns—the old Cleveland Browns—had a great tight end whose name was?"

"Ozzie Newsome," I answered.

"And after the team moved to Baltimore and became the

Ravens, Ozzie Newsome became?" she quizzed me.

"The first African-American general manager in NFL history," I said.

"Very good," she went on, "and Ozzie Newsome played college ball at?"

This one I didn't know, although I should have realized she had already given me a clue. I said, "I don't know. Ozzie Newsome played before I was born. Before you were born."

"So you don't know everything," she snorted. And she turned and started away. This time the hair did that shampoo commercial thing.

I fell in a step behind her. "So?" I asked.

She paused and allowed me to walk up alongside her. "Connect the dots," she said, "and give me a drink of water while you're working on it."

While I was searching for a bottle of water down in the lumpy mess of my backpack, it dawned on me. I had asked her if she was a Ravens fan and she said she was . . . "Alabama," I said, "Ozzie Newsome played for Alabama." I handed her the water.

"Maybe you ain't so dumb after all," she said with the first smile I had seen since the crack of dawn. "But don't get the big head," she continued. "Even if you ain't as dumb as I think, you ain't nowhere near as smart as you think."

She handed me the bottle back without wiping the lip. I didn't wipe it either.

34

THE CHOSEN

Ninety million acres. That's how many acres of longleaf pine there were in North America when Columbus set sail in 1492. Longleaf reigned in the coastal plains of what we now know as the southeastern United States.

Many scientists believe this was the largest ecosystem under one canopy of trees that ever existed in the world. There have been larger ecosystems—rainforests, deserts, oceans, for example. Yet there has never been an ecosystem so dominated by one species of tree. From southern Virginia down through the coastal plains of the Carolinas, Georgia, Florida, Alabama, Mississippi, Louisiana, and on into Texas, longleaf ruled. And how did it exercise dominion over the world around it?

Fire.

Leah told me all of the above when we smelled the fire. We smelled it just a few minutes before we spotted it, because the wind was blowing the smoke away from us. I was ready to turn back into the wind and head away from the fire when Leah said, "This is good news."

"I'm not used to a forest fire being good news," I said.

"Ain't a forest fire; it's a prescribed burn," she corrected me.

"You mean like a doctor wrote a prescription: take two flames and call me in the morning?" I quipped.

That's when she told me about the ninety million acres that longleaf used to dominate through the "use" of fire. "Longleaf is what they call a 'fire adapted species,'" she said. "It can withstand fires and the other trees can't, so the longleaf uses fire to burn out its competition."

"That's sort of anthropomorphic, don't you think?" I asked.

She stopped and stared at me with a look I had seen before. It was the same look she had given me a couple of days before when I said twenty-seven degrees Celsius instead of eighty degrees Fahrenheit. I figured if she was going to lecture me on the longleaf ecosystem, I could return the favor with a vocabulary lesson. "You know what 'anthropomorphic' means, don't you?" I taunted.

"No, but I know what 'know-it-all' means," she jibed back at me.

"Anthropomorphic," I said, trying to sound as much like a know-it-all as possible, "means to attribute human characteristics to non-human things. You said the longleaf 'uses' fire to burn out its competition. That's anthropomorphic."

"But," she retorted, "the longleaf *does* use fire to burn out its competition."

"You're implying that this tree makes a conscious effort to set fires," I said.

"How do you know it doesn't?" she said.

I couldn't believe she would challenge me on this. I said,

"What do you mean, how do I know it doesn't? For crying out loud, it's a tree. It has no fingers. It has no thumb. How do you suppose it strikes a match?"

"Don't need matches," she explained. "The oldest and wisest longleaf pines get together for a council meeting. They call it a 'tree ring.' They choose one from among their own as an offering, a sacrifice. This Chosen One will lift up her branches to the heavens, taunting the very forces of nature. And when nature is sufficiently ticked off, it strikes: three hundred thousand volts surge through the heart of the Chosen One. Her sap—her very life's blood—boils, and her bark cannot contain the love she holds for her fellow longleaf pines. She explodes, sending shining embers of her sacrificing self soaring skyward to then settle softly on the forest floor where pine straw takes up the mission and ignites. Fire burns slowly, steadily devouring everything in its path except the longleaf. And so the longleaf forest is preserved because one of their own has paid the ultimate price."

"In other words," I said, "lightning starts a fire and the longleaf survives while the other trees don't?"

"Yeah, but it sort of loses some of its charm when you put it that way," she said.

"These days it ain't so much lightning strikes as it is the Forest Service that starts the fires," she continued. "They do these prescribed burns at different spots around the forest so they can keep the forest clean and the fires under control."

I was beginning to see how this fire could be good news for us.

"That means," Leah went on to say, "that we're still in the national forest, and there's a possibility there'll be some folks working this fire. Maybe we can bum a ride home."

The smoke of smoldering pine straw began to take on the sweet smell of success as we reached the perimeter of the fire. We were on the western edge of the prescribed burn area. Looking east, north, and south I could see no open flames—just smoke.

"The fire's done its job," Leah said. "They're just lettin' it smolder. Might not be nobody out here now." She sounded as disappointed as I felt.

"Okay," I said, "suppose they're already gone. Which way did they go?"

"Yeah," she said, "if we can find the road they came in and out on, maybe I can figure out where we are."

She strolled out across the smoldering forest floor.

"You're not going to walk out into the middle of a forest fire?" I said.

"Ain't much of a fire no more," she said. She hesitated just long enough to look back at me and say, "You comin' or you stayin'?" then she turned and continued on across the carpet of ash.

Wasn't bad enough that I got hit in the head, wrapped in duct tape and tossed into the back of a pickup truck. Not bad enough I had to jab a guy in the face with an axe. Not bad enough I had to run for my life through a forest at night. Now I had to get my shoes dirty.

35

A SLOW BURN

Three million acres: that's all that's left of the once mighty longleaf kingdom. Prob'ly less than three million. And to make matters worse, what's left of the longleaf ecosystem is fragmented." Leah was telling me all of this as we made our way across the charred ground. I wasn't paying much attention; I was on the lookout for runaway embers. My high-tech nylon hiking pants are great for any hiking situation, or so I thought up until that point. I had never envisioned wearing them in a just-burned longleaf pine forest. These pants were designed to wick away moisture, not red-hot embers. I was thinking how following Leah into the "prescribed burn" area was the dumbest thing I had ever done when it occurred to me that it was the *second* dumbest thing. The dumbest was telling anyone what I had seen out that airplane window.

"Fragmented. You know what 'fragmented' means, don't you?" Leah said.

I knew what it meant. I was too busy to answer. Too busy watching my brown leather boots turn ash-black.

She went on, "For one thing it means a lot of the wildlife is being squeezed into smaller and smaller areas, and . . ."

"Hold on a second," I interrupted her, "it looks to me like a forest fire, prescribed or otherwise, would put the 'squeeze' on the wildlife."

She stopped and raised her left hand as if she were about to conduct an orchestra without a baton. "Look out there," she said while moving the conducting hand in a slow arc that brought forth smoke instead of music. "What do you see?"

She was starting to get on my nerves. I didn't need or want an earth sciences lecture from a Conecuh County know-it-all. What I needed and wanted was a good night's sleep and something to eat besides a stinking granola bar. "I don't see a thing," I said.

"Exactly," she said, "no animals at all. You might think you would see some crispy critters that got caught in the fire."

I wanted to prove her wrong. I wanted to spot a bird, a raccoon, a frog, a lizard, a mouse . . . something . . . anything that had just been barbequed over open flames.

"If the longleaf forest burns regularly it burns slowly," she continued her lecture. "The critters have plenty of time to get out of the way. Some of them even duck down in a gopher tortoise hole and let the fire pass right over the top of them."

She was right, of course, and that irritated me. I don't know why it irritated me; it just did. Maybe it's because I was so ready to be home. Instead, there I was up to my ankles in ash with the occasional swirling cinder threatening the very life of my favorite hiking pants. I said, "What makes you such an expert?"

"I live here," she replied.

She began to walk away. I pulled the straps on my backpack to raise it a little higher on my back and then hitched up my pants and tightened my belt. "Hang on," I said, "I'm coming."

She hesitated long enough for me to come alongside her, and we both walked in silence for several minutes before she said, "Remember when we first met down by Ditch Pond?"

"Sure," I replied.

"Remember how you lectured me with everything you know about alligators?" she asked.

I could see where this was going. I answered anyway, "Yes."

"Well," she said, "now you know how I felt."

"Touché," I said, "and as one know-it-all to another, I have to admit you seem to know what you're talking about when it comes to this forest."

"I'll let you in on a little secret if you promise not to tell nobody, especially my daddy," she said.

I raised my right hand to my mouth and pretended to zip my lip.

"We get a lot of Auburn folks down here," she said. "In fact, Auburn University's got a forestry center, the Solon Dixon Center, kind-a nestled in the northwest corner of this national forest. Lot of students, lot of graduate students come down here to do field work in the national forest. I follow 'em around ever chance I get."

"So why the secret?" I asked.

"'Cause my daddy didn't raise no War Eagles," she said. I had no idea what that meant and was afraid to ask. She kept on as if I knew what she was talking about. "That's why I wear the Raven's sweatshirt," she said. "It's my way of paying respect to the Alabama Crimson Tide without stirrin' up controversy with the Auburn folks."

At this point I realized she was talking about football, and I figured if the rivalry was so intense that you had to be careful of the clothes you wore, it would be best for me to keep quiet about it. We walked on without conversation and without the sounds of millions of organic motors like I had heard in the *un*-burned forest the morning before. Was it just twenty-four hours before that I had heard all of those living engines revving up in the forest around me? Hard to believe. This morning the living creatures—the smart ones, anyway—had all run for their lives. We were left with the clomp of our own footsteps chomping through the snow. At least, that's what it sounded like. The crusty, charred pine straw made a crunching noise like frozen snow. And there was the occasional pop of an exploding twig that sent cinders into the air and nylon fearing for its life. And there was the airplane.

Yep, it was an airplane. A low-flying airplane. Low-flying and slow-flying. It had to be a search plane.

Leah and I both heard it at about the same time. We stopped in our tracks. "Of all the times to be in the middle of a smoldering forest," she said, "wouldn't do a bit of good to make a fire for a smoke signal. We need something to flash, like a mirror or something."

"I have a signal mirror in my backpack," I said, "I just don't think I can get to it."

"Can't get to it!?" Leah was incredulous.

"I didn't have time to repack this morning," I said, "I don't know where anything is down in there."

"Then dump it out!" she screamed, "dump it all out!"

"I paid for this stuff with my own money. I'm not going to . . ." That's about all I got out before she tackled me. She hit me about waist high and we both went down. We rolled over three or four times in the soot before she managed to get me face down and start yanking things out of my backpack. When I managed to get up on my hands and knees, she straddled me like I was some kind of bucking bronco and wrapped her legs around my waist in a scissors hold. I reared up, and over we went. She was on her back with her legs cutting off circulation to my lower extremities, and I could still tell she was jerking stuff from my pack. Overhead the plane was closing in fast. It couldn't have been more than a few feet above the treetops.

"Got it!" yelled Leah. And with that she released me from the death grip.

We both got to our feet at about the time the plane was straight up over our heads. Leah waved the mirror around in the air.

"Quick," I demanded, "give it to me!"

She handed me the mirror without comment or hesitation. I found the sun and sent a beam ricocheting off of the side of the airplane as it zoomed away from us.

The nose of the plane lifted up and it banked to its left and began a turn, a slow turn, a turn that seemed to take forever, a turn back toward us. I flashed him or her or them or whoever was flying the thing a few more times with the mirror. The plane rocked back and forth in a gentle wave, the friendliest wave I've ever seen, a wave that said, "Good to see you!" He or she or they circled us a couple more times just to make sure we knew they knew we were there, and then they flew away. They would send our coordinates to searchers on the ground. All we had to do was stay put. I turned to Leah.

"I could have taken you in a fair fight," I said. "That tackle caught me by surprise."

"Any guy worried about getting his backpack dirty ain't gonna take me fair fight or not," she said. Then she laughed. I thought it was going to be one of those out-of-control laughs like the night before, until she began to cry. It was a gentle weep—slow and steady and cleansing like fire through a longleaf forest.

36

THE LAST LAUGH

We were stuffing the grimy, grungy, grubby contents of my backpack back into the pack when we heard the truck.

"Listen!" said Leah.

"Sounds like it's coming from that direction," I said and pointed toward what I think was the northeast.

"Must be where the road is," she said, " and it can't be that far—maybe fifty yards."

"Let's go!" I yelled. I dropped the backpack and we both took off running toward the road.

"I'm gonna stand in the shower 'til there ain't no more hot water in all of south Alabama," Leah exclaimed.

"What? No bacon and eggs with toast smothered in butter and honey?" I kidded.

"Not unless I can eat without getting' it wet," she answered.

"Look!" I called out, "Look at the dust." It was not smoke from a smoldering forest; it was dust bellowing up from the dirt road as a truck cruised down the road.

"Hurry," Leah insisted, "we got-a get to the road 'fore they blow right by us."

We quickened our pace. Exhausted, we ran on pure adrenaline. We were above the dirt road, and like many of the dirt roads in the Conecuh National Forest, this one had been scraped out, leaving an embankment on each side. That meant we couldn't see the truck as we were running toward it. We saw it soon enough. We scuttled down the embankment and onto the road just as it roared past. It was a pickup. Two-toned, blue and white. Three-toned if you count the rust.

They hit the brakes, and the dust that had been following them rushed past. Leah and I hit our own brakes and turned to scramble back up the bank. We were about to the top when the air erupted with the loudest boom I've ever heard and the ground next to me exploded. Ash and dirt flew up into my face as I reeled to one side. I clipped Leah, and we both tumbled back down to the road. I rubbed soot from my eyes and looked up at Carl Morris. He held a double-barreled shotgun with wisps of smoke spiraling from one of the barrels.

"You was right, Carl," said one of the brothers from somewhere behind him, "that airplane had 'em spotted."

Another brother said, "Yeah, well that airplane gone be sendin' cops out here to get 'em, too. Grab 'em up an' let's get out-a here."

Carl Morris wasn't saying anything, and I could see why. The right side of his face was so swollen that it extended almost out past his shoulder. The face flashed several shades of purple, a couple of weird blues, and a pink that I never would have believed could occur in nature. The right eye was sealed shut. Carl Morris didn't need it. He had enough hate, anger, and meanness for both in his left eye.

"Get up," Carl Morris said to us. At least that's what I think he said. I didn't hear words so much as gurgles. It sounded like he was trying to gargle and talk at the same time—gargle with acid. Drool dripped down the right side of his lip as he spoke.

Leah and I got to our feet. Behind Carl stood his brothers. One was on a crutch he had made out of a tree branch. His left ankle was wrapped in duct tape, and he held it a few inches above the ground as he teetered on his makeshift crutch. The other brother looked to be in pretty good shape considering he was a Morris. This brother shuffled up alongside Carl. Carl handed him the shotgun and gurgled, "Get in the truck."

The brother with the gun used it to motion us toward the back of the pickup. I took a step in that direction, then stopped when I heard Leah say, "We ain't gettin' in that truck Carl Morris. You gonna shoot us, you gonna have to shoot us right here."

Carl muttered, "Shoot 'em."

The brother with the gun moved the barrel back and forth between Leah and me as if trying to decide which of us to shoot first. The brother on the makeshift crutch said, "Only got one shot left. Better make it count. I'd shoot the girl. She's trouble." The shotgun swung toward Leah, then back toward me, then back again toward Leah.

"Sammy Morris," Leah said to the brother with the gun, "if Carl want somebody shot, he ought-a be man enough to do it himself. Ain't no reason for you to sit on death row for somethin' Carl made you do."

Carl didn't wait for his brother Sammy to respond. With abrupt swiftness he pushed between Sammy and Leah, grabbed Leah by the hair and yanked her to the ground.

"You get your hands off of her!" I heard a voice scream—it was my voice. Carl spun around and slammed his forearm across my chest. It knocked me off of my feet, and I hit the ground with a thud that took my breath away. Carl Morris must have stepped over to his truck and reached into the back where he kept his tools, because the next thing I remember was seeing him standing over me with an axe. Yeah, it was the same axe I had jabbed him in the face with the night before.

Carl was not going to jab; he was going to swing. He raised the axe high above his head. I fixed my eyes on the axe head, thinking that maybe I could roll out of the way when the blade came down at me. The blade didn't come as I expected. I heard a loud crack—a gunshot—and the blade lifted up and off of the axe handle and began to spin in midair. Then it began to fall. I scooted backwards just as it slammed into the ground between my legs.

Carl Morris dropped the axe handle and screamed with pain as he staggered away from me. The gunshot had blown the axe head right off and must have reverberated down the handle and through his hands.

From some distance away I heard a familiar voice yell, "Sammy Morris, put that shotgun on the ground and walk away from it, or the next shot will take *your* head off."

I heard Leah say in a small, quiet voice, "Daddy."

Then I heard Sammy Morris say, "Don't shoot, Shirley."

I kid you not. He said, "Don't shoot, Shirley."

I couldn't help laughing. Laughing and laughing and laughing . . .

37

PRESENCE

The Morris brothers will be going away for a long, long time. It turns out that the vehicle I saw three guys pushing into a lake was a Forest Service truck. That means federal charges in addition to the Alabama sins they will have to pay for.

"If they're lucky, they'll get sent to the same prison their daddy's at," said Deputy Pickens. "Be a regular family reunion."

"I'm not sure luck has anything to do with it," said my dad.

"Guess you're right, Professor," said the deputy. "They brought this on themselves."

It was the next morning, and we were sitting around the picnic table at our base camp at Open Pond. There were four of us: my dad, Deputy Shirley Pickens, me and Raymond Marks. Marks, that's what everybody called him, was an Auburn University graduate student. The Forest Service had contracted with him to do a botanical study in the Conecuh National Forest. It was his truck the brothers dumped into the lake.

"All I'm doing is an inventory of the flora—the plants— in the national forest," said Marks. "I don't know why the

Morris boys would've been threatened by that."

"They thought you were looking for red-cockaded wood-peckers," said the deputy. "They got some acreage adjoining the forest, an' you weren't far from there. They were afraid you would find some of the little endangered birds, and they wouldn't be able to cut their timber."

"So they stole my truck and figured I would be lost for-ever in the woods," said Marks. "Fortunately, I had plenty of granola bars in my backpack."

"Granola bars can keep a guy going in a pinch," I said.

"Yeah," said Marks, "I'm known for over-packing, but it came in handy this time." I liked this guy.

I asked Deputy Pickens, "Do you think we'll have to come back to Covington County and testify at the Morris trial?"

"Prob'ly won't be a trial," he replied. "They pretty much got caught red-handed. Prob'ly make some kind of plea bargain."

"If they're smart," said my dad.

"Ain't nobody ever accuse them of being smart," said the deputy.

My dad got up and poured coffee for everyone except me. I got myself an orange juice from the cooler. We all sat and sipped in silence for a few minutes. A slight breeze moved across the water, through our camp and up into the forest where a presence danced across the tree tops tickling the longleaf pine needles. It made a sound, some would say, like wind chimes way off in the distance. Others, those in the know, would say it sounded like bacon frying. *I'm lying in my bed, and my momma's in the kitchen frying up some eggs and bacon—beef bacon. The sound reaches me before the smell does, but soon I'll smell it, too, and then I won't be able to stay in bed no longer. Eggs and bacon and toast with lots of butter and honey."*

Deputy Pickens broke the silence when he spoke to my dad. "I appreciate your wife letting Leah tag along with her this morning," he said. "I've always told her that if you want-a be smart, you got-a hang around with smart people."

"Yeah," said my dad, "I'm sure that's why my wife wants to hang around with Leah."

I nodded in silent agreement.

ABOUT THE AUTHOR

Roger Reid is a writer, director, and producer for the award-winning *Discovering Alabama* television series, a program of The University of Alabama's Alabama Museum of Natural History in cooperation with Alabama Public Television. He lives with his family in Birmingham.

———————————————

To learn more about Conecuh National Forest
and the plants and animals found there,
and for news of Jason and Leah's further adventures,
visit **www.rogerreidbooks.com** or
www.newsouthbooks.com/rogerreid

MORE JASON CALDWELL ADVENTURES FROM ROGER REID

Space and *Time*

Young sleuth Jason Caldwell returns in *Space* and *Time,* author Roger Reid's sequels to *Longleaf.* In *Space,* Jason must determine which of his father's "Space Cadets" astronomer friends is a spy—or worse—at their annual reunion at the Marshall Space Flight Center in Huntsville, Alabama, In *Time,* Jason and Leah must dodge old enemies among the fossils at the Steven C. Minkin Paleozoic Footprint Site in north Alabama—the richest source of vertebrate trackways of its age in the world. Roger Reid's novels combine real-life locations and scientific fact with engaging, multi-layered whodunit mysteries.

Available in hardcover and ebook

WWW.NEWSOUTHBOOKS.COM/ROGERREID

Space: ISBN 978-1-58838-230-6

Time: ISBN 978-1-58838-262-7